awkward

Svetlana Chmakova

awkward

✧ SVETLANA CHMAKOVA ✧

Coloring assistants: Ru Xu, Melissa McCommon

Lettering: JuYoun Lee

150 West 30th Street, 19th Floor
New York, NY 10001

Visit us at yenpress.com
facebook.com/yenpress
twitter.com/yenpress
yenpress.tumblr.com
instagram.com/yenpress

First JY Edition: July 2015

JY is an imprint of Yen Press, LLC.
The JY name and logo are trademarks of Yen Press, LLC.

The publisher is not responsible for websites (or their content) that are not owned by the publisher.

Library of Congress Control Number: 2015945195

Hardcover ISBN: 978-0-316-38132-1
Paperback ISBN: 978-0-316-38130-7

10 9 8 7

LSC-C

Printed in the United States of America

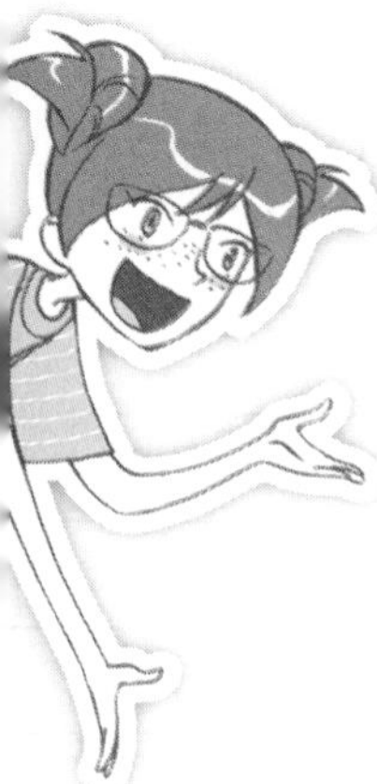

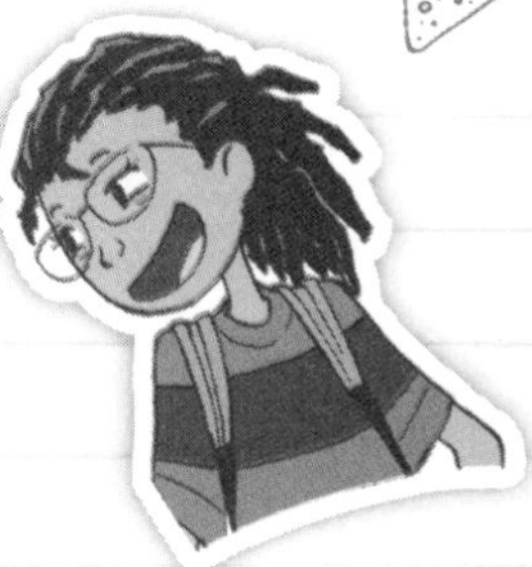

Table of Contents

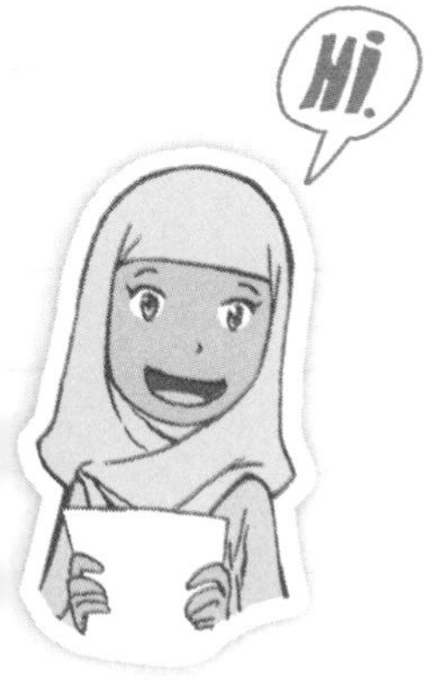
Hi.

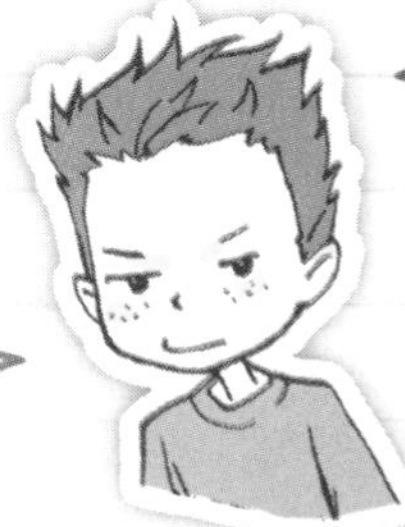

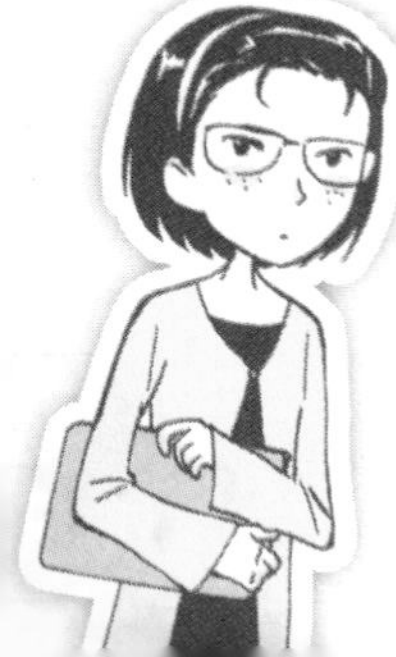

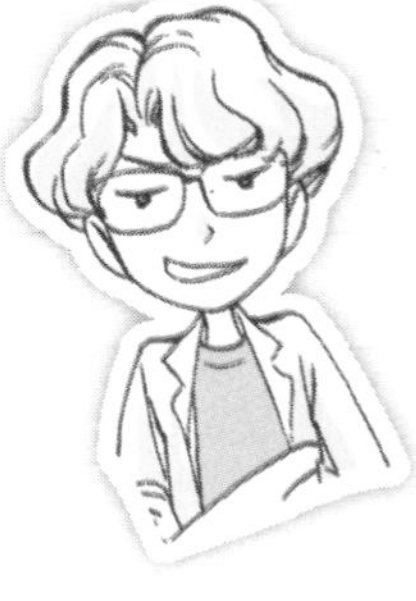

CHAPTER 1

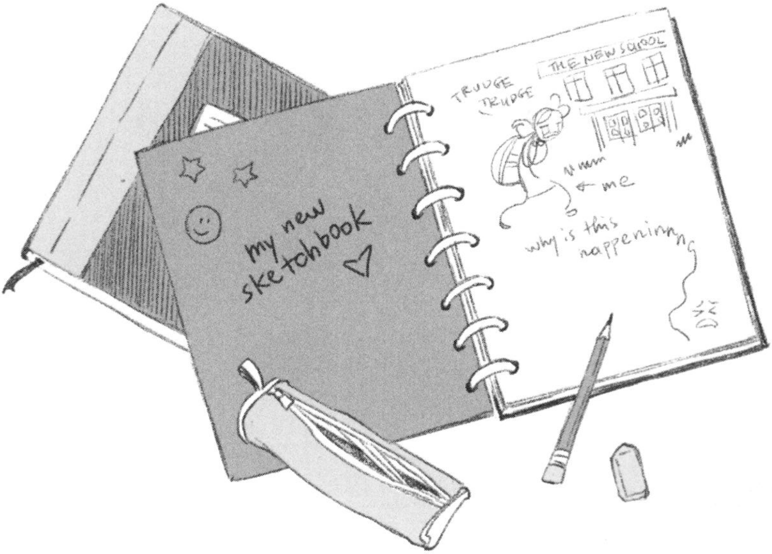
my new sketchbook
THE NEW SCHOOL
TRUDGE TRUDGE
← me
why is this happeninnng

OKAY, SO WHEN YOU'VE JUST MOVED TO A NEW TOWN AND ARE STILL A TOTAL OUTSIDER...

...THIS...→

TRIP

WAH!!

...IS **NOT** THE BEST WAY TO START LIFE AT YOUR NEW SCHOOL.

HI! PENELOPE HERE. PEPPI FOR SHORT.

IT'S MY FIRST DAY AT BERRYBROOK MIDDLE SCHOOL, AND I JUST TRIPPED OVER MY OWN FEET AND DROPPED **EVERYTHING.**

INCLUDING MY DIGNITY.

HA HA HA HA HA HA

AND THEN THIS BOY COMES OVER TO HELP.

WHICH IS SWEET AND KIND OF GREAT, RIGHT?

EXCEPT...

HA HA HA

NERDER FOUND A NEW GIRLFRIEND!

HA HA

HEY, NERDER, WHEN YOU GUYS GET MARRIED, IS SHE GONNA COOK YOU DINNER IN TEST TUBES?

....!!

CARDINAL RULE #1 FOR SURVIVING SCHOOL: DON'T GET NOTICED BY THE MEAN KIDS.

HAHAHAHA

NERDER GIRLFRIEND.

NERDER GIRLFRIEND.

FAIL.

BIG FAIL!!

...AND THEN...

HERE.

I DID SOMETHING THAT STILL MAKES ME BURN.

LEAVE ME ALONE!

PUSH

HAHAHAHAHA

TURN

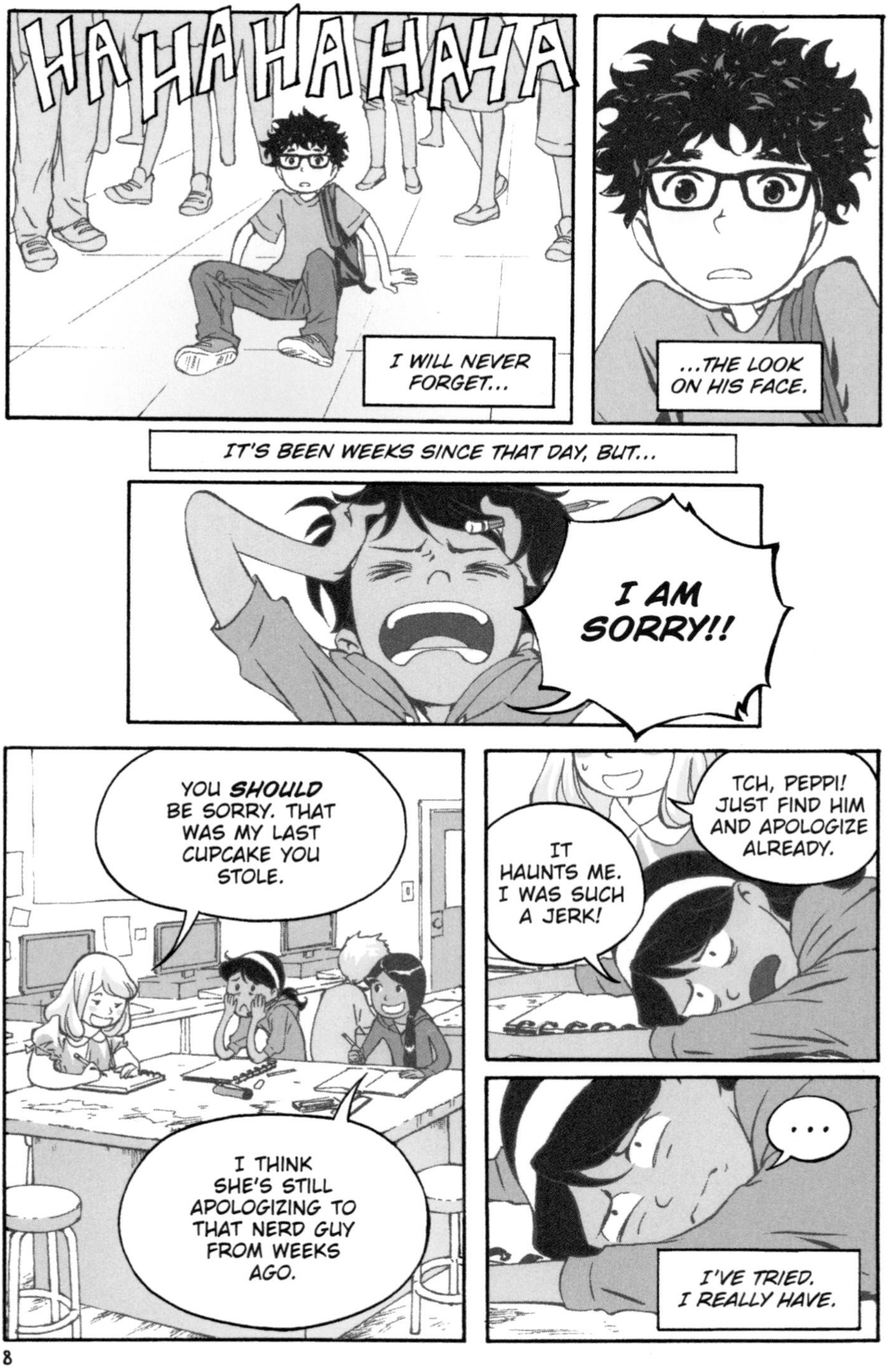
HAHAHAHAHAHA
I WILL NEVER FORGET...
...THE LOOK ON HIS FACE.
IT'S BEEN WEEKS SINCE THAT DAY, BUT...
I AM SORRY!!
YOU SHOULD BE SORRY. THAT WAS MY LAST CUPCAKE YOU STOLE.
I THINK SHE'S STILL APOLOGIZING TO THAT NERD GUY FROM WEEKS AGO.
IT HAUNTS ME. I WAS SUCH A JERK!
TCH, PEPPI! JUST FIND HIM AND APOLOGIZE ALREADY.
...
I'VE TRIED. I REALLY HAVE.

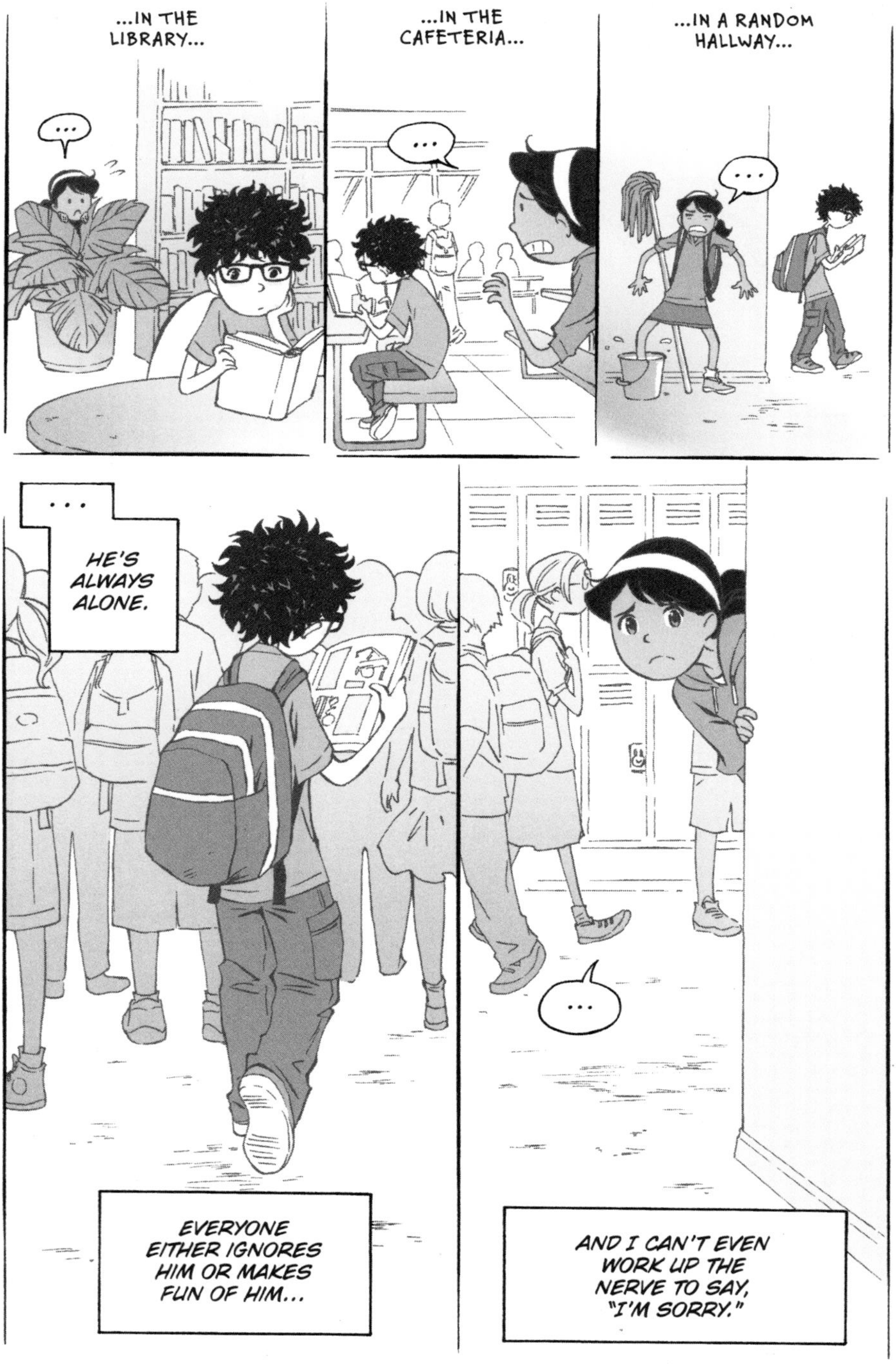
...IN THE LIBRARY...
...
...IN THE CAFETERIA...
...
...IN A RANDOM HALLWAY...
...
...
HE'S ALWAYS ALONE.
...
EVERYONE EITHER IGNORES HIM OR MAKES FUN OF HIM...
AND I CAN'T EVEN WORK UP THE NERVE TO SAY, "I'M SORRY."

I can't dooooooo it...

He probably hates meeee...

I can't face thaaaaat...

MISS TORRES, I DID NOT CALL THIS EMERGENCY ART CLUB MEETING TO DISCUSS YOUR MORAL DILEMMAS!

TAP TAP TAP

!

I HAVE MOST DISTRESSING NEWS.

IS IT THE SUNSPOTS ARE THEY FINALLY

IT'S NOT THE SUNSPOTS, JENSEN! SIT BACK DOWN!

IT'S MUCH WORSE.

WORSE THAN SUNSPOTS?

AS YOU ALL KNOW, EACH SPRING THE SCHOOL HOLDS THE...

ANNUAL SCHOOL CLUB FAIR

THAT MAGICAL TIME WHEN CLUBS EMERGE FROM THEIR DAILY TOILS...

...TO BASK IN THE LIGHT OF APPRECIATION FROM THEIR FELLOW STUDENTS.

GLAMOUR!

RECOGNITION!

...THE AWARD FOR THE BEST TABLE...

...BUT THIS YEAR...

SLUMP

...OUR BELOVED ART CLUB...

...WILL NOT GET A TABLE.

WHAAAAAT?!!

OH YES. I SHOULD EXPLAIN THIS. CARDINAL RULE #2 FOR SURVIVING SCHOOL: SEEK OUT GROUPS WITH SIMILAR INTERESTS AND JOIN THEM.

I LIKE TO DRAW, SO...

ME

...I JOINED THE ART CLUB!

ART!

THIS IS OUR SUPERVISING TEACHER, MR. RAMIREZ...

...AND YOU KNOW WHO DOES GET A TABLE?!

...BUT IT'S MORE LIKE WE'RE HIS SUPERVISING CLUB.

THE SCIENCE CLUB!!

BOOOO!!

12

WE HAAAAAATE THE SCIENCE CLUB.

THEY'RE ACROSS THE HALL FROM US, ALWAYS CAUSING TROUBLE...

HA HA HA HA HA

HSSSS

SCIENCE ROOM

...BUT THEY ALWAYS GET AWAY WITH IT BECAUSE THEY WIN AWARDS AND MAKE THE SCHOOL LOOK GOOD.

HA HA HA HA

THE ONLY NOTABLE THING THE ART CLUB HAS DONE IS DESIGN THE SCHOOL'S FOOTBALL TEAM LOGO.

BERRYBROOK WIENER DOGS

(AND... UM...THE FOOTBALL TEAM DIDN'T LIKE IT.)

MURMUR *GRUMBLE*

THAT'S SO UNFAIR.

STUPID SCIENCE CLUB.

BUT WE ALREADY STARTED!

IT'S **ALWAYS** THE SCIENCE CLUB! THEY GET ALL THE RESOURCES... WHAT ARE WE GOING TO DOOOO?

DON'T WORRY, MR. R.

PAT PAT

WE'LL FIGURE SOMETHING OUT.

MARIBELLA SAMSON. CONFIDENT, TALENTED, PROBLEM-SOLVER. AND A GO-GETTER.

I'D HATE HER IF I DIDN'T KIND OF WANT TO *BE* HER.

THE SPIRIT OF THE ANNUAL CLUB FAIR IS THAT *ALL* CLUBS RECEIVE EQUAL RECOGNITION FOR THEIR HARD WORK! IT IS *OUTRAGEOUS* TO EXCLUDE A CLUB!

O-OUTRAGEOUS! YES, YES!

WE WILL FIGHT THIS...

...AND WE WILL WIN!

YEEEEEAAAH!

MAN, MARIBELLA SURE IS SOMETHING.

I KNOW, RIGHT?!

BERRYBROOK MIDDLE SCHOOL

SHE'S LIKE SOME UNSTOPPABLE FORCE OF NATURE.

A TORNADO OF GETTING THINGS DONE!

...

I WISH I WERE A TORNADO-LIKE FORCE OF NATURE.

...BUT I'M MORE LIKE A TINY DRAFT...

HEY, PEPS, DO YOU WANT TO GO SEE THE—

15

...HUH? WHERE'D SHE GO? SHE WAS JUST HERE.

THAT GIRL IS LIKE A NINJA, I SWEAR.

HEY, PEPS!

PENELOPEEE!

C'MON. LET'S GO HOME!

. . .

ANOTHER MORNING.

ANOTHER SCHOOL DAY.

RR RING

LATE LATE LAAAAATE

AND NOW IT'S TIME FOR...

...MORNING ANNOUNCEMENTS! THE SCHOOL FOOTBALL TEAM WILL BE PLAYING —

YOU DIDN'T FINISH YOUR SCIENCE HOMEWORK?!

ARE YOU CRAZY?!

I KNOW, I KNOW!! I GOT CARRIED AWAY DRAWING A MERMAID FOR ART CLASS!

...DON'T YOU HAVE SCIENCE FIRST THING TODAY AFTER HOMEROOM?

Y-YES...

...I-IT'S OKAY! I JUST HAVE TO QUICKLY FINISH THIS DIAGRAM NOW, AND...

...WHO AM I KIDDING I AM SO <u>DEAD</u>. she's going to feed me to the venus flytrap noooooo

I KNooooow...

AW, GEEZ! HERE! COPY MINE!

PEPPI, YOU HAVE TO TAKE SCIENCE MORE SERIOUSLY!! SHE'LL FAIL YOU— SHE TOTALLY WILL!

A-ALL ART CLUB MEMBERS! WE'RE MEETING AFTER SCHOOL AGAIN TODAY!

YOU'LL COME, RIGHT?

DID YOU FINISH IT?

K-KINDA? I THINK...?

OKAY, WE'VE GOT MATH NOW. GOOD LUCK, PEPPI!

THANKS.

DON'T BECOME PLANT FOOD!

THE LUCK... I NEED IT.

SCIENCE CLASS... IS NOT FOR THE MEEK-HEARTED.

NOT SO MUCH THE CLASS ITSELF, BUT...

...THE TEACHER.

SCREEE

THEY SAY...

...THAT SHE MASTERED KUNG-FU AT AGE NINE...

...AND GRADUATED UNIVERSITY AT AGE THIRTEEN.

RUMOR GOES THAT SHE WAS TELLING **NASA** WHAT TO DO AT EIGHTEEN.

I HAVE NO IDEA HOW MUCH OF THAT IS TRUE...

GOOD MORNING, CLASS.

...BUT I'M READY TO BELIEVE **ALL** OF IT.

MEET MISS TOBINS, OR MISS T WHEN SHE'S IN A GOOD MOOD.

GULP

SHE IS THE SUPERVISING TEACHER OF THE SCIENCE CLUB.

IT'S POSSIBLE SHE ALSO RUNS THE WORLD IN HER SPARE TIME.

I HOPE EVERYONE FINISHED THE DIAGRAM ASSIGNMENT BECAUSE I'M GOING TO COLLECT THEM NOW...

...AND MARK THEM WHILE YOU WORK ON THIS SURPRISE QUIZ.

LET'S SEE HOW MUCH YOU'VE LEARNED.

PAT PAT

NoOOoOoOOoOo...!

TIC TOC TIC TOC

RRRING

NOOOO, I'M NOT DONE FAILING MY QUIZ YET!

COME ON, PEPPI. THE NEXT CLASS IS COMING IN NOW.

J-JUST ONE MORE MINUTE!

?

!!

PACK PACK

SLINK SLINK

PLACE

MISS TORRES!

MAY I SEE YOU FOR A MOMENT?

I HAVE A QUESTION ABOUT THE BONUS MATERIAL YOU INCLUDED WITH YOUR SEA LEVEL DIAGRAM ASSIGNMENT.

I WASN'T SURE WHAT TO MAKE OF IT.

HUH?

BONUS MATERIAL...?

THIS.

GAH!!

I, UH!

THAT'S A MISTAKE!

GRAB

GRAB

IT'S FOR ART...I WAS JUST...

MISTAKE? *NONSENSE.*

THIS COULD EASILY BE A SCIENCE PROJECT.

TELL ME, HOW DOES THIS WORK BIOLOGICALLY?

DOES SHE BREATHE AIR, LIKE DOLPHINS?

OR DOES SHE HAVE GILLS, LIKE FISH?

WHAT'S HER SKELETON LIKE? IS IT HALF-FISH, HALF-HUMAN?

UH.

UM.

EH?

WILL YOU DRAW A DIAGRAM AND LABEL IT FOR ME?

BONUS MARKS!

...U-UH. ...OKAY ...?

GREAT.

NOW, THERE'S JUST ONE MORE THING I WANTED TO DISCUSS WITH YOU, PENELOPE.

23

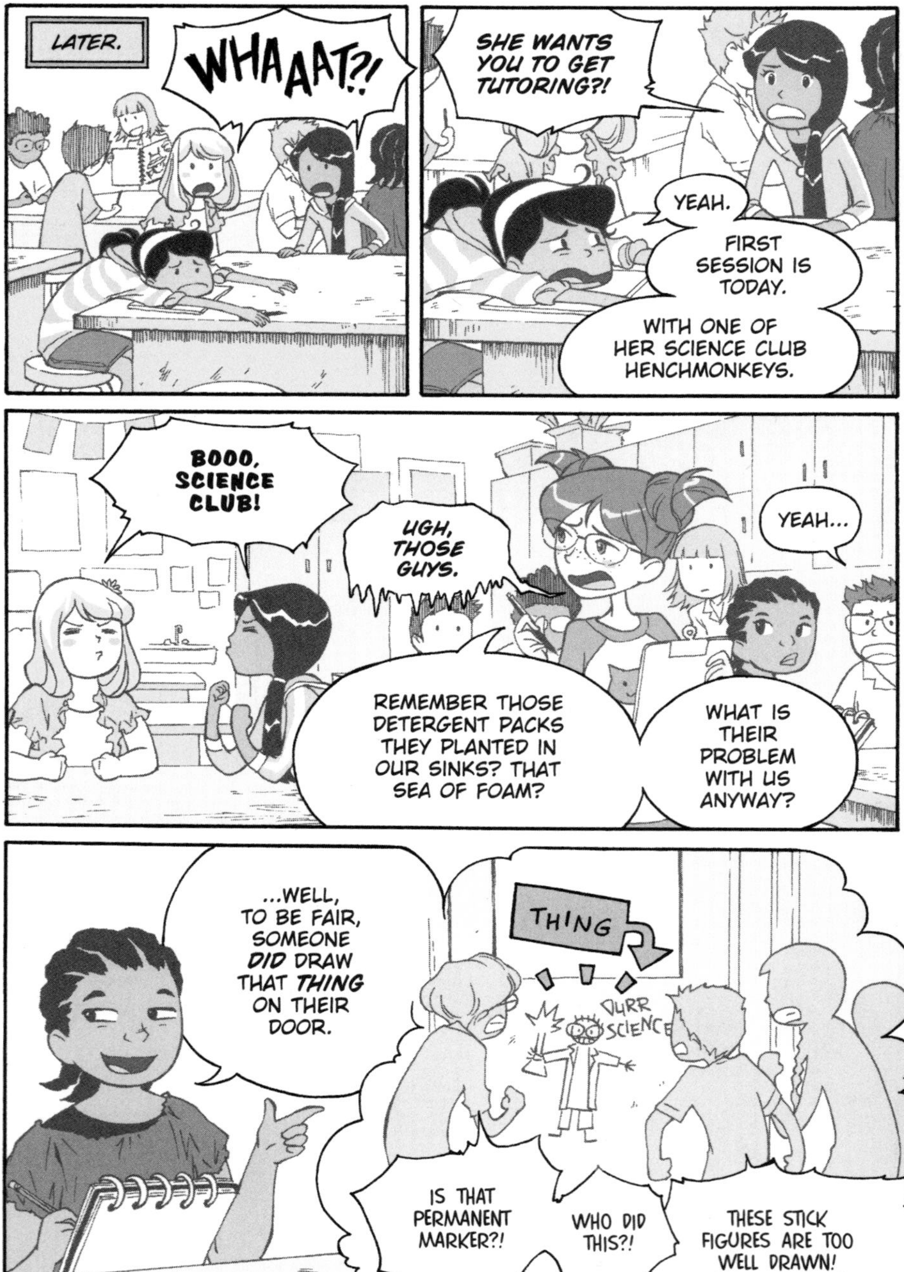
LATER.
WHAAAT?!
SHE WANTS YOU TO GET TUTORING?!
YEAH.
FIRST SESSION IS TODAY.
WITH ONE OF HER SCIENCE CLUB HENCHMONKEYS.
BOOO, SCIENCE CLUB!
UGH, THOSE GUYS.
YEAH...
REMEMBER THOSE DETERGENT PACKS THEY PLANTED IN OUR SINKS? THAT SEA OF FOAM?
WHAT IS THEIR PROBLEM WITH US ANYWAY?
...WELL, TO BE FAIR, SOMEONE DID DRAW THAT THING ON THEIR DOOR.
THING
DURR SCIENCE
IS THAT PERMANENT MARKER?!
WHO DID THIS?!
THESE STICK FIGURES ARE TOO WELL DRAWN! IT'S GOT TO BE THE ART CLUB!!

PLEASE, THEY HAD *NO PROOF* THAT WAS US!

WHO EVEN KNOWS WHO IT WAS?

HEH HEH HEH

IT WASN'T EVEN THAT GOOD A DRAWING!

MAYBE IT WAS JUST...SOMEONE ELSE WHO THINKS THEY'RE ALL DORKS.

BARGE

HERE THEY ARE, MARIBELLA!

COPIES, LIKE YOU ASKED!

...BUT I ONLY ASKED FOR TWENTY.

O-OH! I MADE EXTRA COPIES, JUST IN CASE.

HE ACCIDENTALLY PRESSED AN EXTRA ZERO.

MAYBE WE CAN BUILD A PAPER JET.

WELL, ANYWAY, THANK YOU, MR. R.

LET'S BEGIN.

LISTEN UP, ART CLUB!

YES, YES! LISTEN!

I WENT TO THE PRINCIPAL'S OFFICE TODAY.

I DEMANDED AN EXPLANATION FOR THE INJUSTICE OF DENYING US A TABLE AT THE FAIR...

...AND THIS IS WHAT HE SAID TO ME.

PRINCIPAL

WELL, MISS SAMSON, I HATE TO SAY THIS, BUT...

...THE ART CLUB DOESN'T REALLY DO ANYTHING.

WHAAAAAT?!!

YES, YES, THAT IS WHAT HE SAID.

AND I HATE TO SAY THIS, BUT...

...HE'S RIGHT.

WE'VE DONE **NOTHING** TO CONTRIBUTE TO THE SCHOOL COMMUNITY.

WHEN THE DRAMA CLUB ASKED US TO PAINT THE STAGE BACKDROPS — WHAT HAPPENED?

ER...

UM...

ERM...

NO ONE STEPPED UP, THAT'S WHAT HAPPENED!

AND THAT WASN'T THE ONLY TIME!

EVERYONE IS ALWAYS BUSY PLAYING GAMES OR DOODLING THEIR OWN THINGS.

IF WE WANT TO BE PART OF THE SCHOOL'S CLUB SCENE...

...**WE HAVE TO CONTRIBUTE.**

...SO HOW'RE WE GONNA DO THAT?

. . .

UM.

HMM...

WELL...

...IS IT TOO LATE TO HELP THE DRAMA CLUB?

YES.

WHAT IF WE PAINTED A MURAL FOR THE SCHOOL?

WE COULD DO CONCEPTUAL ART INSTALLATIONS ON THE FOOTBALL FIELD!

I SAW THIS DOCUMENTARY, AND THEY USED THESE GLASS BUBBLES TO—

OH, UM, ACTUALLY...

...WE...WE DON'T HAVE THE BUDGET FOR ANYTHING BIG...

AWWW...

B-BUT MARIBELLA HAS A GREAT IDEA! SHE—

PLEASE, MR. R, LET'S HEAR EVERYONE FIRST!

OOPS!

C'MON, GUYS! IDEAS!

SOMETHING THAT'S CHEAP TO MAKE BUT WILL BE NOTICED BY THE WHOLE SCHOOL!

HMMMMMM

MUMBLE   CHATTER   MURMUR

...   ...

mumble

mumble

Hmm, maybe art...for the newspaper...?

WHAT WAS THAT, PENELOPE? YOU'RE SO QUIET!

...!

FLINCH

DO YOU HAVE AN IDEA?

WHAT IS IT? SPEAK UP!

...

u-uh...

E-EVERYONE'S LOOKING AT MEEEE...

DO. NOT. LIKE.

...IT'S NOTHING. IT'S STUPID...

WHAT'S YOUR IDEA, MARIBELLA?

WELL...

I WAS PRETTY **MIFFED** AT WHAT THE PRINCIPAL SAID.

SO I SPENT THE REST OF THE DAY THINKING, WHAT COULD WE DO?

WHAT'S A PROJECT THAT'S **NOTICEABLE**, BENEFICIAL TO THE SCHOOL COMMUNITY, **AND** SOMETHING ONLY THE ART CLUB CAN DO?

AND THEN IT OCCURRED TO ME THAT...

...OUR NEWSPAPER? IT HAS **NO ART** IN IT!

....!

...SHE'D GIVE US A FULL PAGE.

SO I TALKED TO JENNY, THE NEWSPAPER EDITOR, AND ASKED HER IF SHE'D GIVE US SPACE TO CONTRIBUTE...

...AND SHE SAID THAT AS LONG AS WE REFLECT SCHOOL LIFE IN OUR ART...

WHAAAT! WOOOOAH!! A PAGE IN THE NEWSPAPER?!

INTRODUCING...

COMIC PUNCH!

ART CLUB PRESENTS COMIC PUNCH! (MOCK-UP ISSUE)

by Maribella Samson

...THE SCHOOL PAPER'S *FIRST EVER* COMIC STRIP FEATURE ABOUT SCHOOL LIFE!

SO...WHO HERE WANTS TO GET PUBLISHED?

YEEAAH!

...I...

...I REALLY SHOULD'VE SAID SOMETHING. REALLY, REALLY.

OH MAN, OH MAN, THIS IS GONNA BE AMAZING! I CAN'T WAAAAIT!!

WHATCHA GUYS GONNA DRAW, WHATCHA GONNA DRAW?

MY STORY'S GOING TO BE ABOUT ADDING ROBOTS TO THE CAFETERIA...

MWAH HA HA

...AND THEN THEY MALFUNCTION AND TAKE OVER THE SCHOOL! FOODPOCALYPSE!

WHAT, NO SUNSPOTS?

I COULD MAKE A COMIC ABOUT SUNSPOTS I COULD WARN EVERYBO

TESS, WHY...

SORRY, COULDN'T RESIST.

THE WORLD MUST KNO

WELL, MY COMIC'S GONNA HAVE ACTUAL SCHOOL LIFE FACTS. MY STUPID SISTER'S IN THE SCIENCE CLUB, SO I'M GONNA—

SCI...!

MY SCIENCE TUTORING SESSION!!

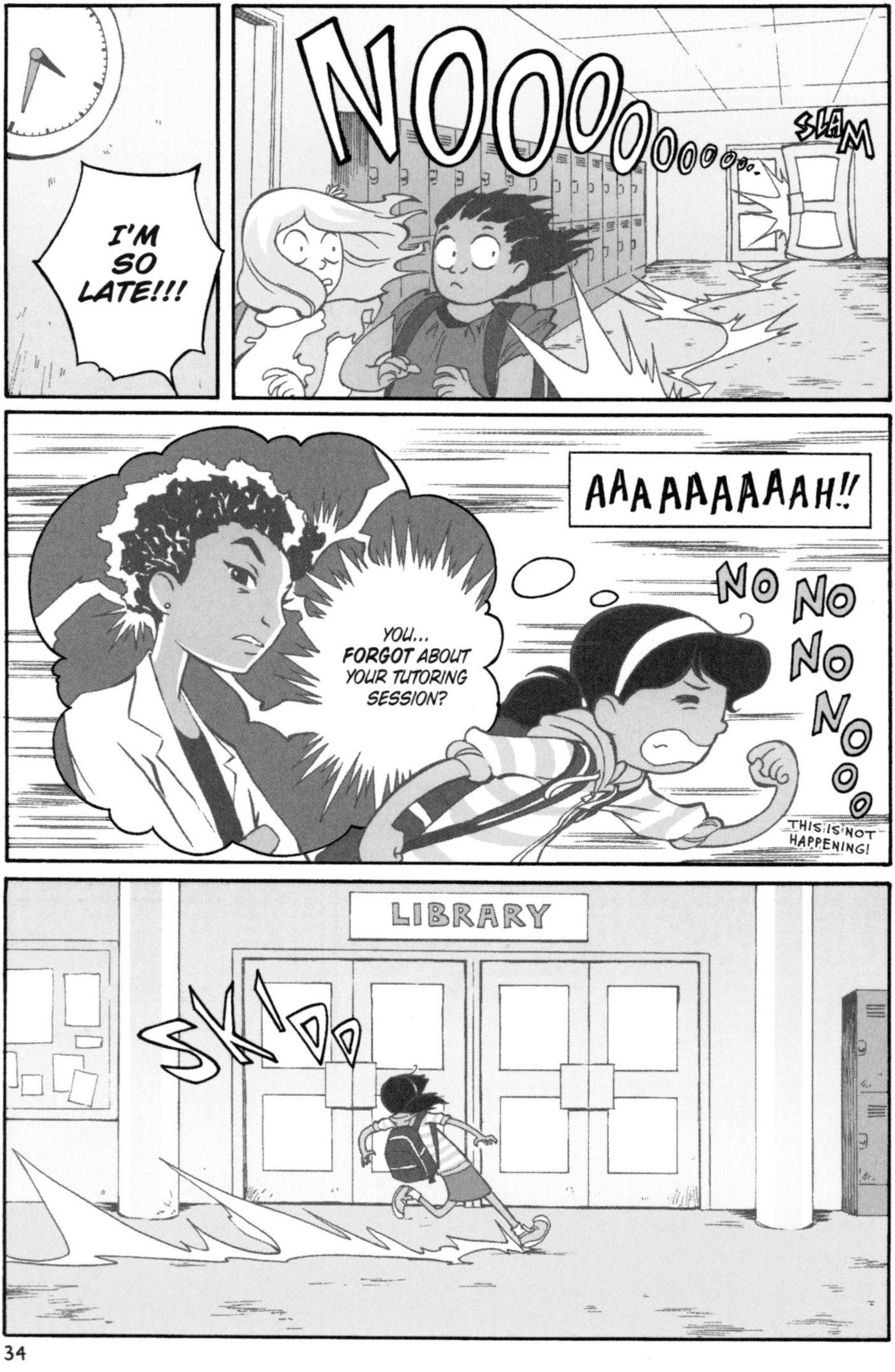
I'M SO LATE!!!
NOOOOOOOOOO...
SLAM
AAAAAAAAAH!!
YOU... FORGOT ABOUT YOUR TUTORING SESSION?
NO NO NO NOOOO
THIS IS NOT HAPPENING!
LIBRARY
SKIDD

HUFF HUFF

IT'S EMPTY?!

MRS PRATT IS THERE ANYONE FROM THE SCIENCE CLUB I WAS LATE AND

YES, HE'S JUST IN THE BACK, IN THE COMPUTER AREA.

DASH

THANK YOU!!!

SKIDD

HELLO! SORRY I'M LA—

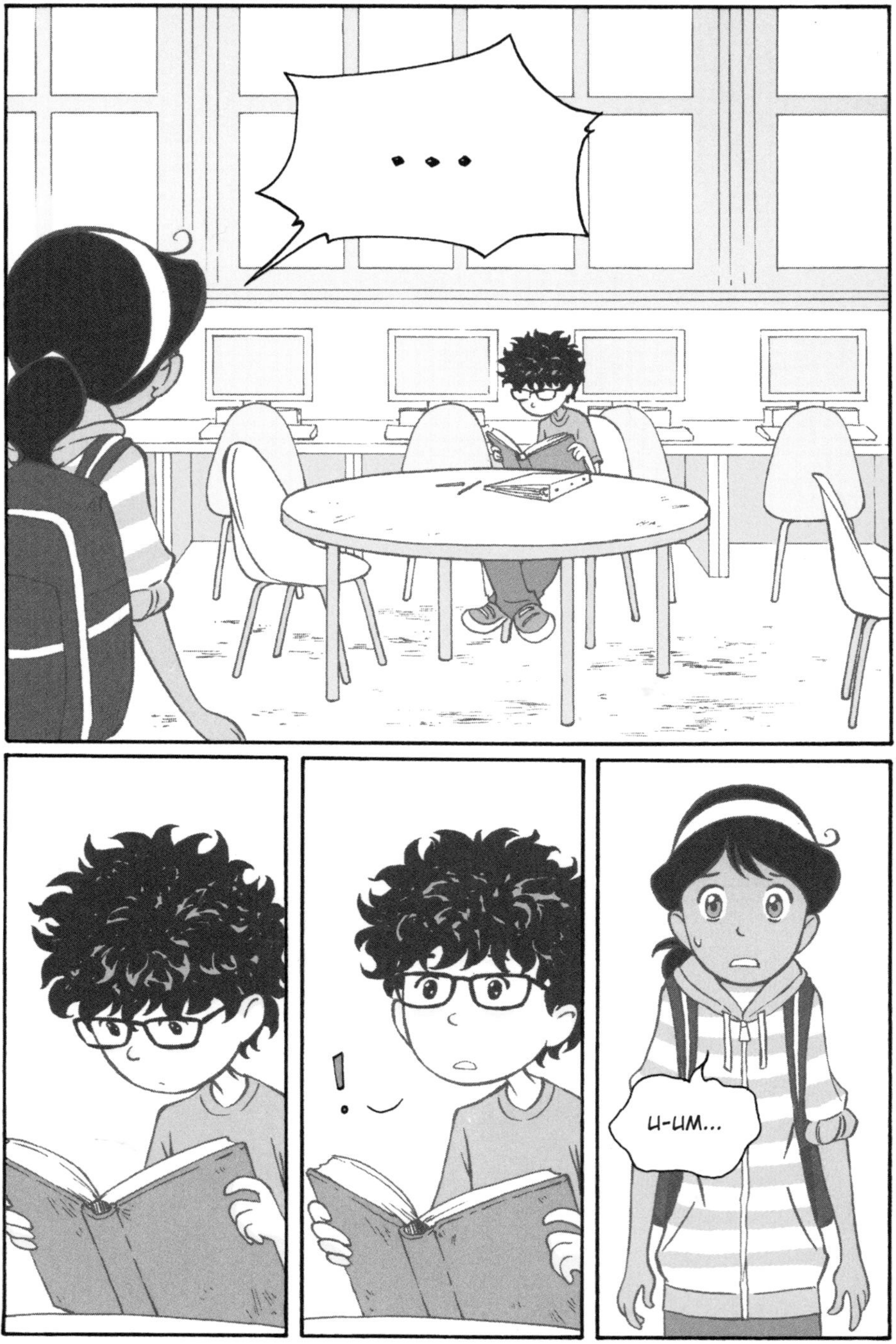
...
!
U-UM...

CHAPTER 2

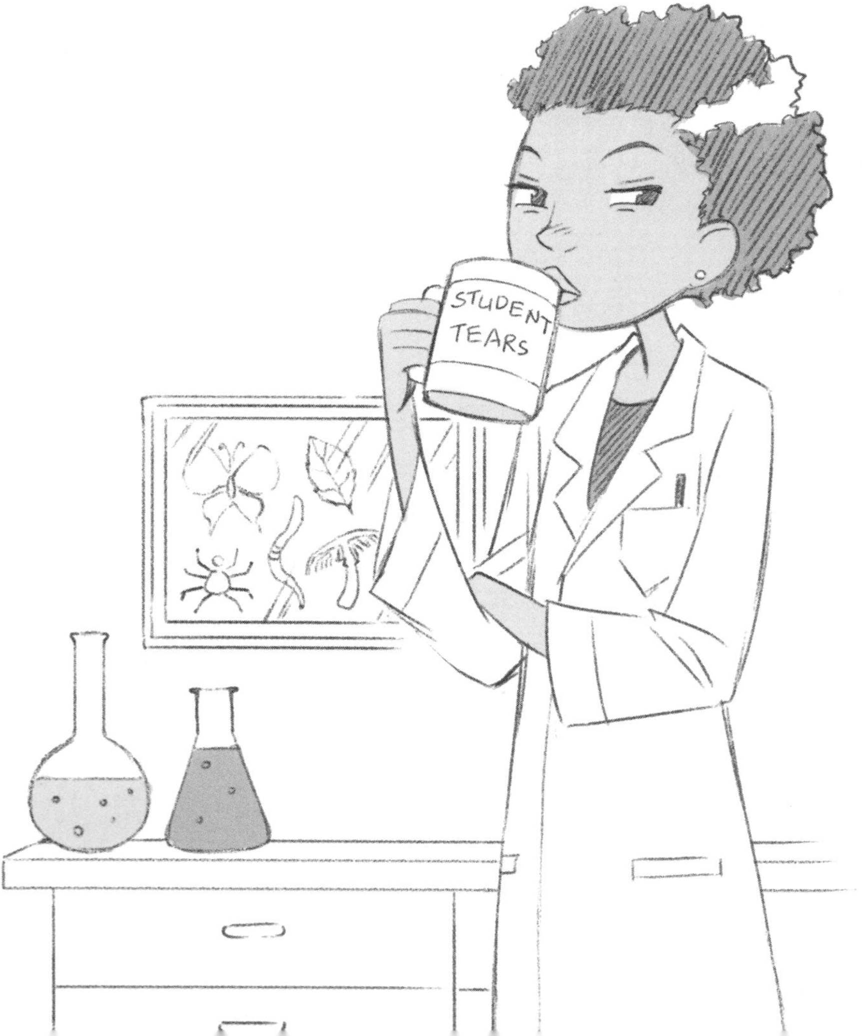
STUDENT
TEARS

Awkward *adj.*
1. *...THIS.*

H-HE...HE'S JUST SITTING THERE. NOT SAYING ANYTHING.

SHOULD I SAY SOMETHING?

...I SHOULD *APOLOGIZE.*

"I'M SORRY I PUSHED YOU."

...HE PROBABLY HATES ME SO MUCH RIGHT NOW.

HERE.

A LIST OF TOPICS WE SHOULD COVER.

DO YOU HAVE ANY QUESTIONS...

...

...DO YOU HATE ME?

...ABOUT YOUR HOMEWORK?

...OH.

WELL... UM...

MISS TOBINS SAID THAT...

...SHE WANTS TO SEE A SCIENCE-Y DIAGRAM OF *HER*.

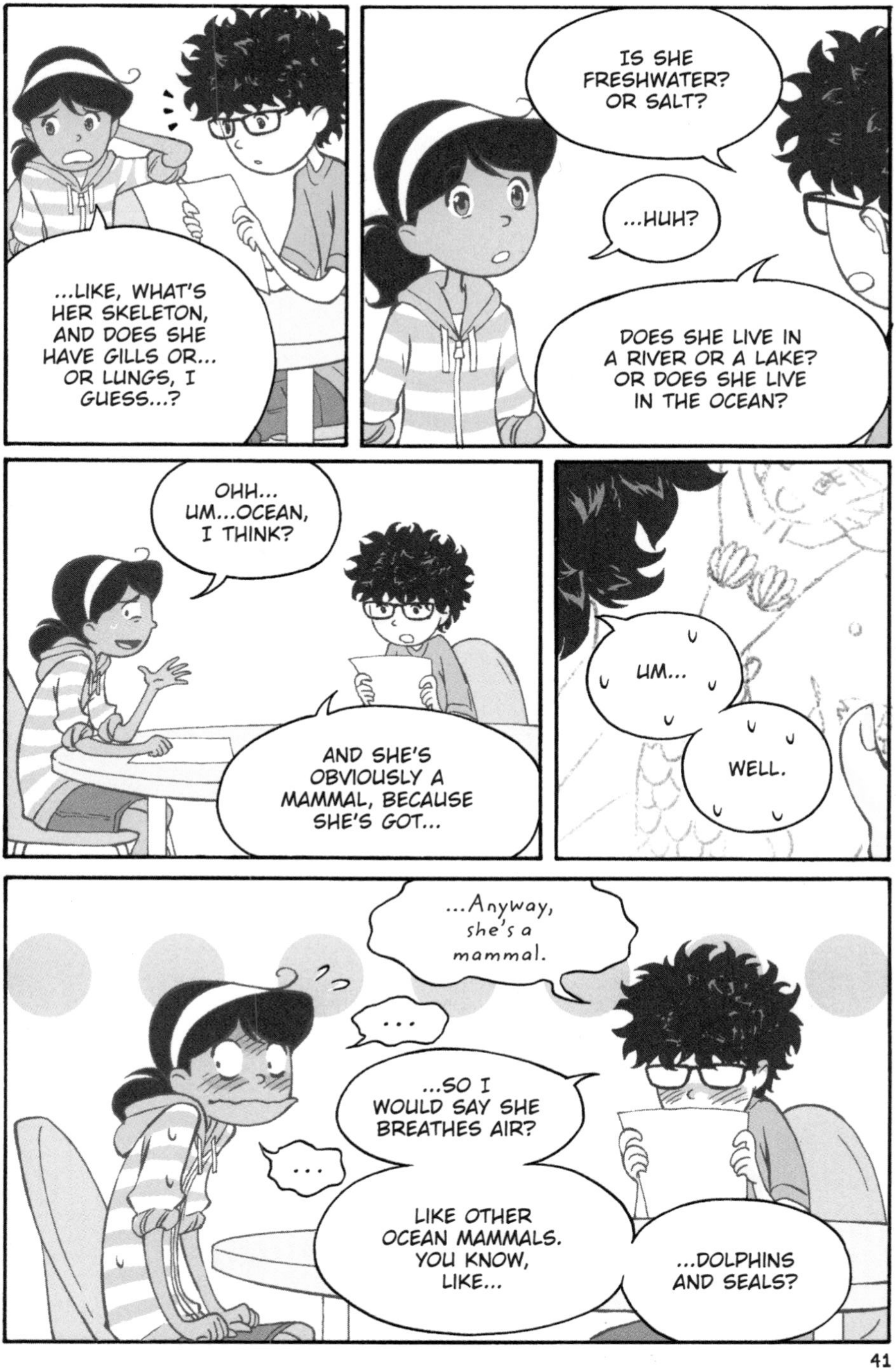
...LIKE, WHAT'S HER SKELETON, AND DOES SHE HAVE GILLS OR... OR LUNGS, I GUESS...?
IS SHE FRESHWATER? OR SALT?
...HUH?
DOES SHE LIVE IN A RIVER OR A LAKE? OR DOES SHE LIVE IN THE OCEAN?
OHH... UM...OCEAN, I THINK?
AND SHE'S OBVIOUSLY A MAMMAL, BECAUSE SHE'S GOT...
UM...
WELL.
...Anyway, she's a mammal.
...
...SO I WOULD SAY SHE BREATHES AIR?
...
LIKE OTHER OCEAN MAMMALS. YOU KNOW, LIKE...
...DOLPHINS AND SEALS?

UM, YEAH.

YES.

SURE.

SO HERE'S A LIST OF THINGS WE'LL NEED TO LOOK UP...

...

... ...

LIST OF THINGS TO NEVER PUT IN A SCIENCE ASSIGNMENT EVER AGAIN: *1. MERMAID DRAWINGS.*

TIC TOC

TIC TOC

LIBRARY

IS THAT ENOUGH INFO?

Y-YEAH, I CAN LOOK UP THE REST AT HOME.

UM...

THANKS VERY MUCH FOR HELPING ME.

...

TURN

....!

...HE DOES HATE ME?!!

AAAAAAAA

42

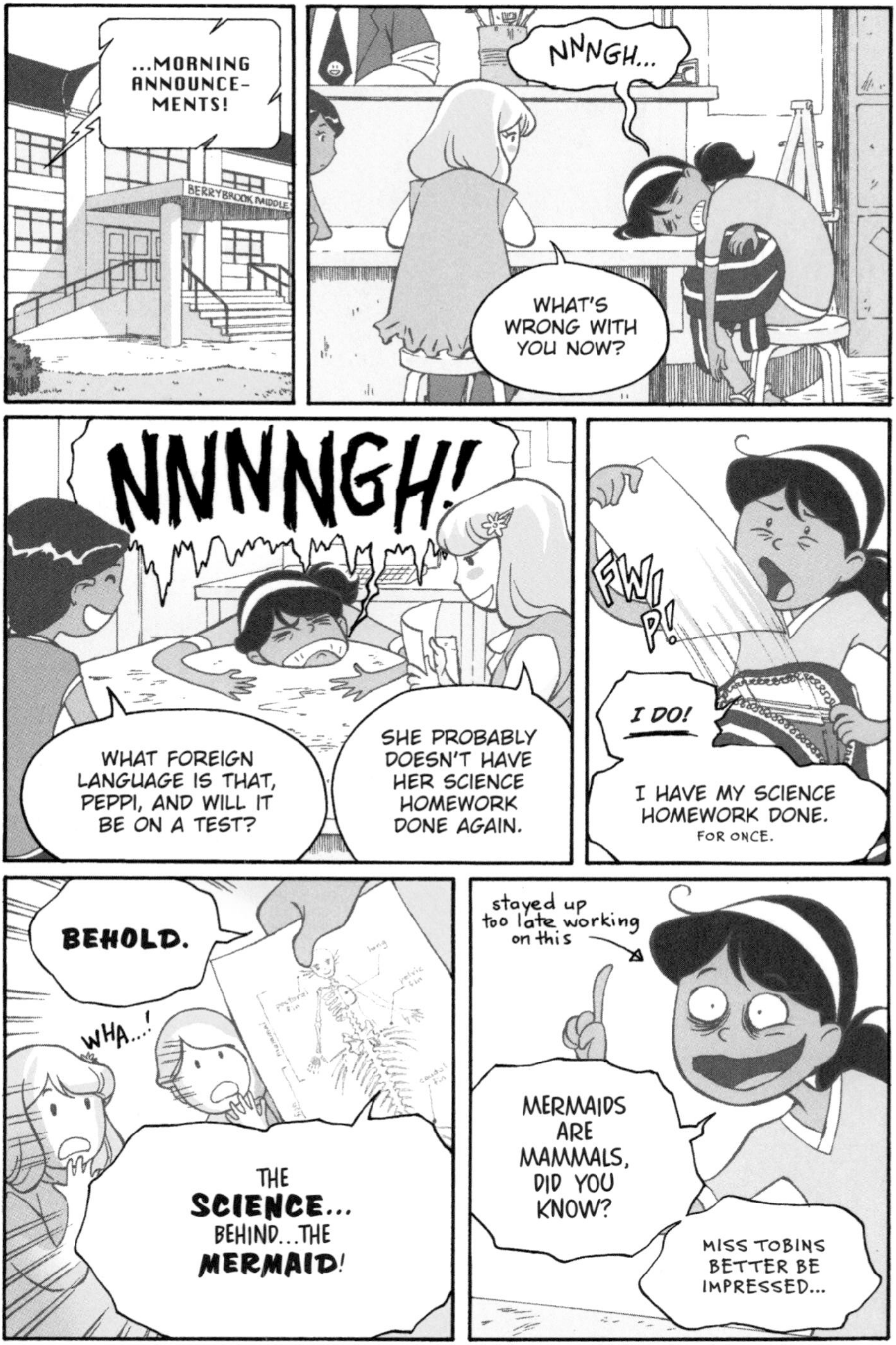
...MORNING ANNOUNCE-MENTS!
BERRYBROOK MIDDLE
NNNGH...
WHAT'S WRONG WITH YOU NOW?
NNNNGH!
WHAT FOREIGN LANGUAGE IS THAT, PEPPI, AND WILL IT BE ON A TEST?
SHE PROBABLY DOESN'T HAVE HER SCIENCE HOMEWORK DONE AGAIN.
FWIP!
I DO!
I HAVE MY SCIENCE HOMEWORK DONE. FOR ONCE.
BEHOLD.
WHA...!
THE SCIENCE... BEHIND... THE MERMAID!
stayed up too late working on this
MERMAIDS ARE MAMMALS, DID YOU KNOW?
MISS TOBINS BETTER BE IMPRESSED...

RRRING

...MISS TORRES, I AM VERY IMPRESSED.

OH GOOD...

THANK YOU.

I SEE YOUR TUTORING SESSION WAS VERY PRODUCTIVE. YOU AND JAIME GOT ALONG WELL, THEN?

OH, UM...

GOOD. I'LL SCHEDULE ANOTHER SESSION FOR NEXT WEEK.

....!

...AAAAAAAAAAAAAAA

EVERYONE, DON'T FORGET YOUR FIELD TRIP PERMISSION SLIPS.

...THE PROBLEM WITH HAVING FRIENDS ONLY IN YOUR CIRCLE OF INTERESTS...

...IS THAT, OUTSIDE OF THAT CIRCLE?

YOU'RE ON YOUR OWN.

MATH CLASS.

MUSIC CLASS.

GYM.

...ART CLUB!

I MISSED YOU GUUUUYS.

HA-HA, WHAT? YOU JUST SAW US THIS MORNING!

DID YOU THINK OF MORE STORY IDEAS?

DID I? MATH WAS SO BORING, I ALMOST WROTE A NOVEL!

RUSTLE

I FINISHED MINE.

SLAM

THE TRUTH ABOUT SUNSPOTS.

UH, JENSEN...

...THAT'S TOO MANY PAGES.

LET'S TALK ABOUT THE FORMAT, GUYS! I MADE A TEMPLATE!

HERE THEY ARE, MARIBELLA! COPIES!

.....!

NOOOO, I ONLY ASKED FOR TWENTY...

MR. R!!

E-EXTRAS! YOU JUST NEVER KNOW!

SERIOUSLY, A JET. LET'S DO IT.

I CAN'T SHORTEN THIS IT IS IMPORTANT

TESSA, THIS IS YOUR FAULT.

I KNOOOW.

BZZZ

BZZZZZ

BZZZZZ

?

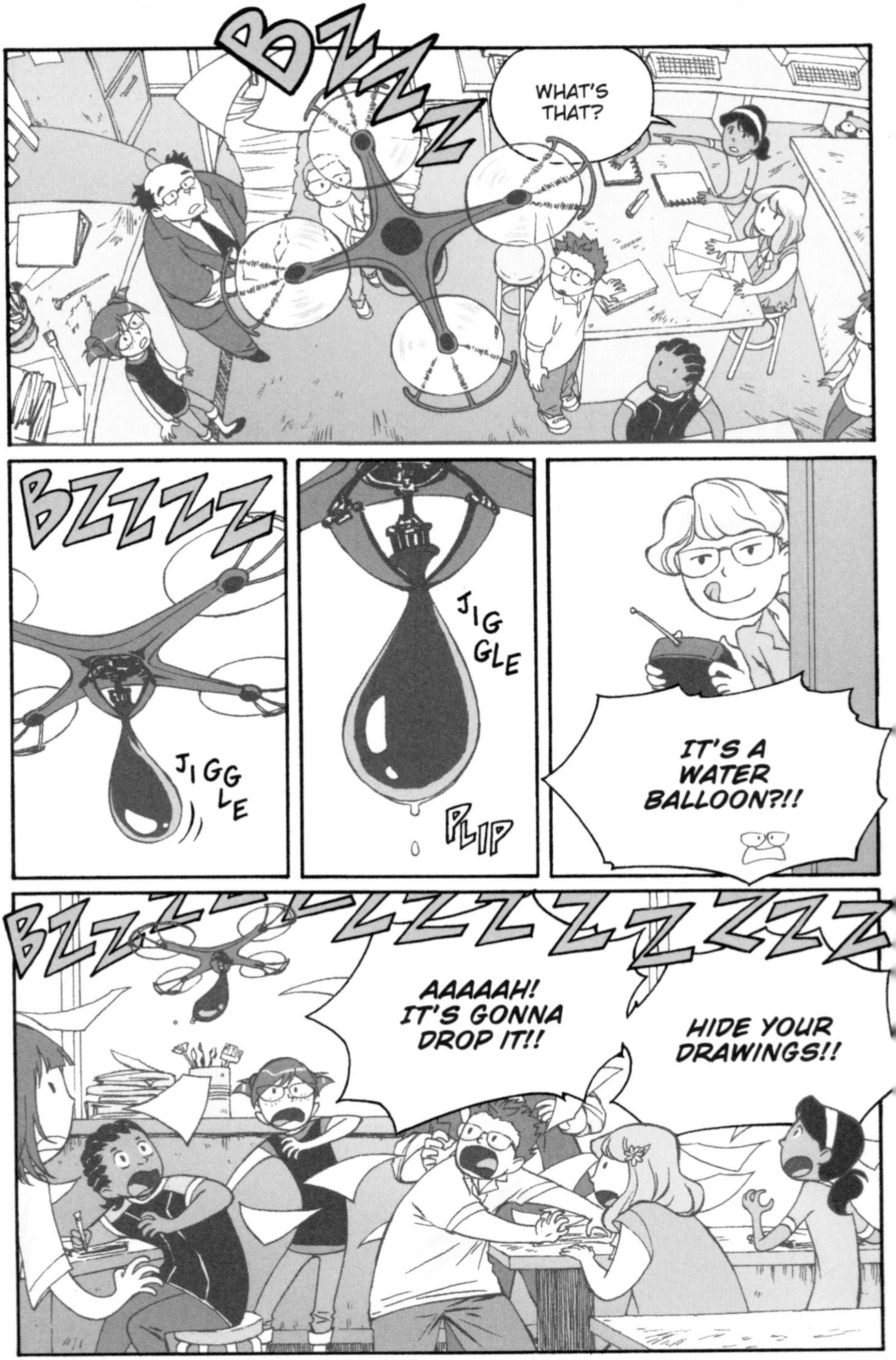
BZZZZ
WHAT'S THAT?
BZZZZZ
JIGGLE
JIGGLE
PLIP
IT'S A WATER BALLOON?!!
BZZZZZZZZZZZZZZZ
AAAAAH! IT'S GONNA DROP IT!!
HIDE YOUR DRAWINGS!!

HEE HEE HEE

DON'T YOU DARE!

SHOO!!

GO AWAY!! GO AWAY!!

BZZZ

JIGGLE

AAAAA

MR. R, YOU HAVE TO DO SOMETHING!!

WHAT? ...OH! RIGHT!

...

ART ROOM

MISS TOBINS, YOU HAVE TO DO SOMETHING!!

WHAT.

GAH!

WHY ARE YOU YELLING, DOMINIC? I'M *BUSY.*

Y-YOUR... YOUR CLUB!! C-CAUSING TROUBLE!

IS THIS TRUE?

NO, NO, MERELY AN EXPERIMENTAL FLIGHT THAT WENT OFF-COURSE.

AH!

AN EXPERIMENT! WHAT ARE THE FINDINGS, MR. LEE?

WELL, WE TIMED THE FLIGHT WITH THE WEIGHT AND WITHOUT, SO THE DATA FOR COMPARISON IS...

UH-HUH, UH-HUH.

HEH HEH HEH

GRRRRR

grumble grumble

?

DORK

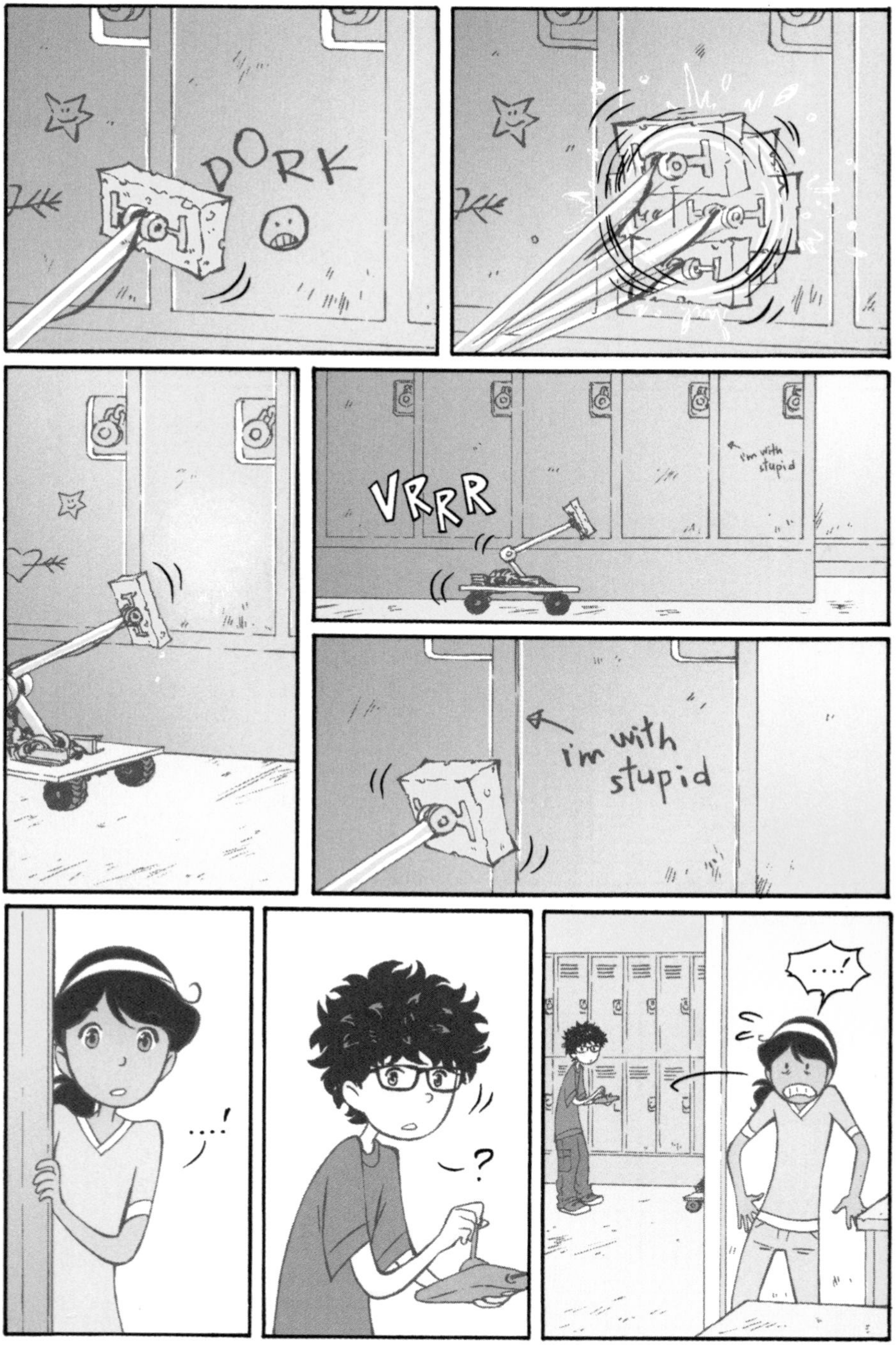
DORK
VRRR
i'm with stupid
i'm with stupid
...!
?
...!

PENELOPE!

GAH!

CAN I TALK TO YOU FOR A SECOND?

ABOUT WHA—

HERE'S THE COMIC STRIP TEMPLATE.

LET ME KNOW IF YOU HAVE QUESTIONS.

ALSO, WOULD YOU LIKE TO BE MY CO-EDITOR FOR "COMIC PUNCH"?

. . .

WHAT?

ME?

WHYYY...?

YOU'VE GOT A GOOD EYE. AND GOOD IDEAS.

I HEARD YOU THE OTHER DAY, YOU KNOW.

WHEN YOU HAD THE IDEA TO PUT ART IN THE NEWSPAPER?

...

AAAAAAAAAA...

C'MON, C'MON, EDIT WITH ME! IT'LL BE FUN!

TWIST

...

EVERYONE!! MEET MY NEW CO-EDITOR!

WAIT, WHAT?

SHE'LL DO THINGS SO THAT YOU DON'T HAVE TO!

...OKAY.

SWEET!

CHIRP CHIRP

BERRYBROOK MIDDLE SCHOOL

...MORNING ANNOUNCE-MENTS!

WHY DID I AGREE?

AWW, WHAT'S SO BAD ABOUT THAT?

WELL, NOW I HAVE TO DRAW MY COMIC **AND** HELP EDIT.

AND I STILL DON'T EVEN HAVE AN IDEA I LIKE!

YOU'LL COME UP WITH SOMETHING.

THE SCIENCE FIELD TRIP IS TODAY! MAYBE YOU'LL GET INSPIRED.

by Penelope Torres

i don't know wut to write

??

ARGH!

HMM... MAYBE...

UGH.

HALF THE SCIENCE CLUB DORKS ARE HERE TOO.

...

HEH HEH

OH, HEY, ART CLUB!

GOOD LUCK SQUEEZING EDUCATION INTO THAT SINGLE BRAIN CELL OF YOURS!

UUUGH.

C'MON, GUYS. LET'S GO IN.

HELLO, EVERYONE!

WELCOME TO THE DISCOVERY CENTER!

I WAS TOLD THAT YOU ARE STUDYING ECOSYSTEMS, SO WE PREPARED A SPECIAL PRESENTATION FOR YOU!

PLEASE MEET JASON NGUEN, OUR GUEST SPEAKER FOR TODAY.

'SUP.

JASON IS A FAMOUS TRAVEL WRITER AND GLOBE-TROTTER.

YOU NAME AN ECOSYSTEM— JASON'S PROBABLY BEEN CLOSE ENOUGH TO TOUCH IT.

SOMETIMES *TOO* CLOSE.

I GOTTA SAY, GATHERING SAMPLES FROM AN ACTIVE VOLCANO...PROBABLY NOT SMART.

A VOLCANO?! DID YOU *SEE* ANY LAVA?

SAW ENOUGH LAVA TO LAST A LIFETIME, YEAH. AND PROBABLY BEAT A FEW RECORDS FOR RUNNING.

OKAY, EVERYONE, GRAB A SEAT BY THE SCREEN, AND MR. NGUEN WILL SHOW YOU SOME OF THE PLACES HE'S SEEN!

. . .

...I DON'T KNOW HOW LONG HE TALKED FOR...

...BUT IT FELT LIKE WE WENT AROUND THE WORLD.

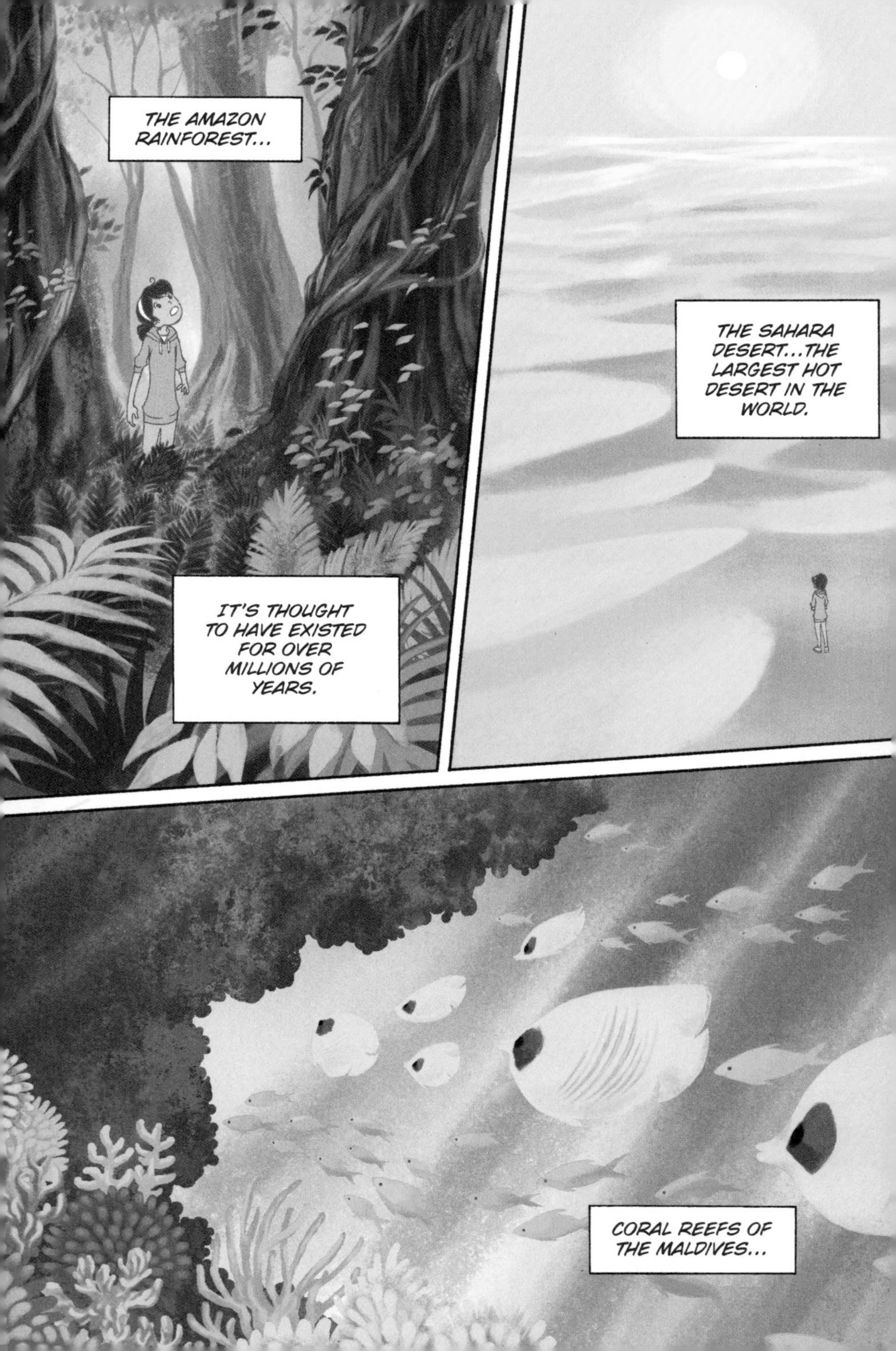
THE AMAZON RAINFOREST...
IT'S THOUGHT TO HAVE EXISTED FOR OVER MILLIONS OF YEARS.
THE SAHARA DESERT...THE LARGEST HOT DESERT IN THE WORLD.
CORAL REEFS OF THE MALDIVES...

THE ARCTIC...

HANG SO'N ĐOÒNG —
THE WORLD'S
LARGEST CAVE.

TEPUI (TABLE-TOP
MOUNTAINS) —AN ISOLATED
ECOSYSTEM MILES ABOVE
GROUND LEVEL.

...WOW.

...ONE PERSON CAN GO SEE ALL THAT...?

...SO THAT POLAR BEAR SURE LEARNED HIS LESSON THAT DAY!

...AS DID I, BUT LET'S NOT DWELL ON THAT.

...AAAND THAT'S IT FROM ME!

...BUT I BELIEVE THERE'S AN ADVENTURE THAT YOUR TEACHER HAS PLANNED FOR YOU.

YES, THANK YOU VERY MUCH, JASON.

ALL RIGHT, EVERYONE, WHO HERE CAN TELL ME WHAT GEOCACHING IS?

OH!

?? ??

LETICIA?

IT'S KINDA LIKE A GLOBAL SCAVENGER HUNT—THERE ARE THESE CONTAINERS, *GEOCACHES*, HIDDEN ALL OVER THE WORLD.

IF YOU HAVE THE RIGHT COORDINATES, YOU CAN USE A GPS TO GO AND FIND THEM.

CORRECT!

NOW, HERE WE HAVE A FEW GPS DEVICES...

...AND ON THE GROUNDS OF THE DISCOVERY CENTER, WE'VE HIDDEN FIVE GEOCACHES WITH MYSTERIOUS CONTENTS.

BUT! TO FIND OUT THE COORDINATES...

...YOU HAVE TO SOLVE A SERIES OF FIENDISH SCIENCE PUZZLES I'VE DESIGNED.

...Ugh, scavenger hunt?

What are we, five...?

MISTER FOSTER.

MISTER YANIC.

THE ALTERNATIVE IS DUSTING FOSSILIZED ANIMAL **EXCREMENT** SAMPLES IN THE CENTER'S **EXTENSIVE COLLECTION**...

...FOR THE **NEXT HOUR**. DID I JUST HEAR YOU VOLUNTEER FOR THE JOB?

N-NO!

GOOD.

...NOW, YOU WILL ALL DIVIDE INTO FIVE TEAMS AND USE **TEAMWORK** TO SOLVE THE PUZZLES.

THE LOCATIONS ARE MARKED ON YOUR MAP...

...AND YOU HAVE ONLY FORTY-FIVE MINUTES TO SOLVE THEM!

TEAM ONE, OVER THERE.

TEAM TWO.

TEAM THREE AND TEAM FOUR.

AND LAST BUT NOT LEAST...

...TEAM FIVE!

READY...

SET...

SNICKER

GO!

OKAY, THE FIRST PUZZLE IS IN THE ARCTIC WILDLIFE SECTION, EXHIBIT B-14!

HELLO, TEAM FIVE!

YOUR FIRST PUZZLE IS: "THE FIRST IS THE NUMBER OF MAMMALS YOU SEE. THE SECOND IS BIRDS THAT FLY OVER THE SEA."

OH, OH!!

IT SAYS HERE THAT THESE ARE *MIGRATORY BIRDS!!*

ONE, TWO, THREE...

saunter

OKAY, GOT IT!

GOOD THING WE GOT STUCK WITH THE *NERD SQUAD.*

THEY'LL SOLVE EVERYTHING, AND WE WON'T HAVE TO DO A THING.

HA-HA, YEAH.

HEY, NERDS! DO MY HOMEWORK NEXT!

...

...

HA HA HA

GOOD ONE

CLICK

OKAY, NEW PLAN. WE HAVE ONLY FORTY-FIVE MINUTES, AND TO WIN, WE NEED TO DO THIS FAST.

WE'LL COVER MORE GROUND IF WE SPLIT UP, SO...

...YOU TWO SMART GUYS TAKE THE PUZZLE IN THE TERRARIUM WING...

?

...AND WE'LL TAKE THE REST.

WAIT, WHAT?

What's a terrarium?

HA HA HA

I DIDN'T KNOW THIS PLACE HAD A TERRARIUM!

UM...IT DOESN'T.

WHICH THEY'LL FIND OUT SOON, I GUESS.

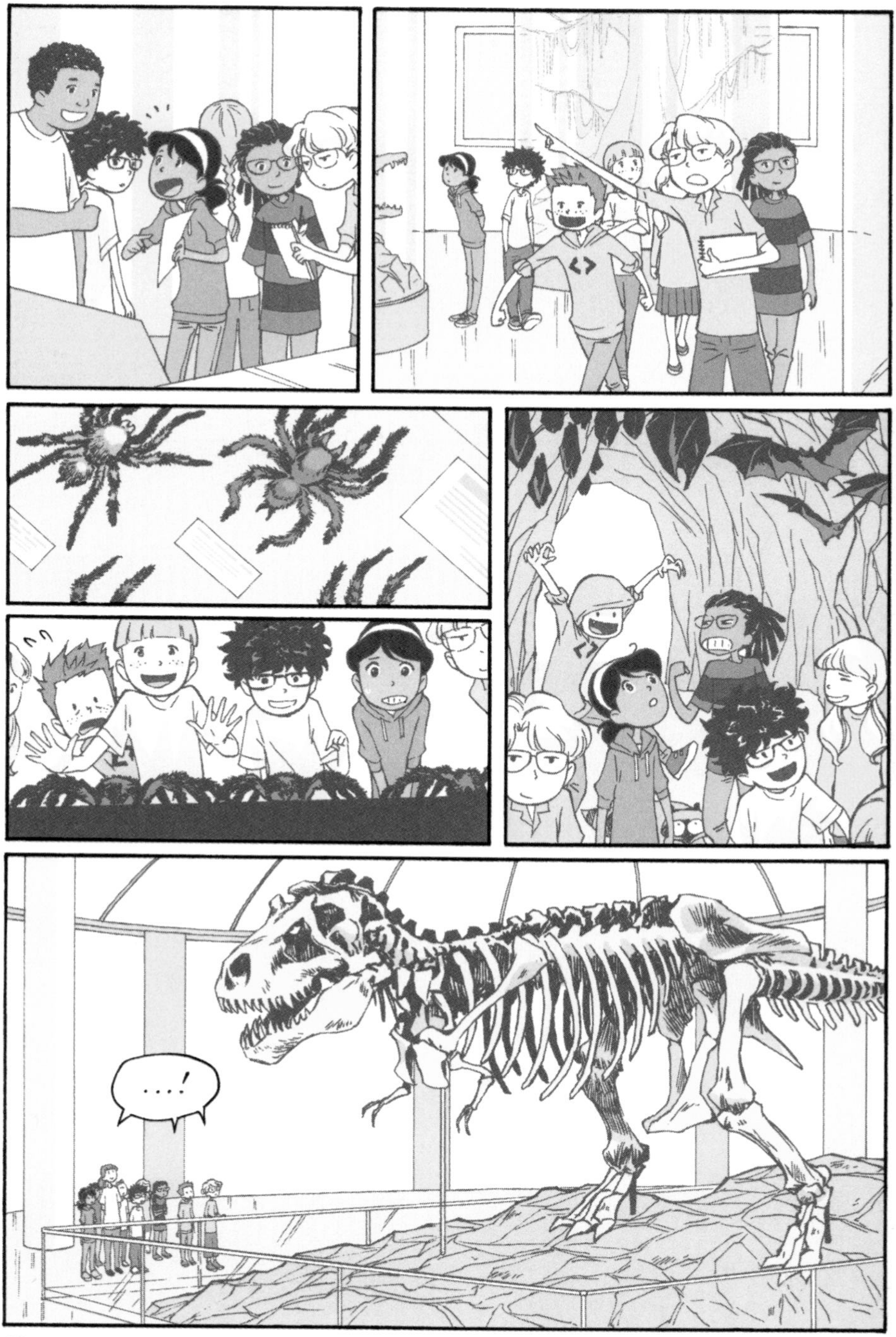
....!

CONGRATULATIONS, TEAM FIVE!

YOU'RE THE FIRST ONES TO FIGURE OUT ALL YOUR COORDINATES!

NOW YOU HAVE JUST TEN MINUTES TO FIND YOUR GEOCACHE!

GO GO GO!!!

WHERE IS IT?! ARE WE CLOSE?!

IT SAYS IT'S ABOUT TWENTY FEET THAT WAY!

TEAM FIVE, YOU HAVE SEVEN MINUTES LEFT!

THE HINT FOR THE CACHE IS: "ONE OF THESE THINGS IS NOT LIKE THE OTHERS."

SEARCH

SEARCH

WHERE IS IT?!

LOOK

I DON'T SEE ANYTHING!

LOOK

C'MON, GUYS, WE MUST BE SO CLOSE!

KNOCK

KNOCK

THREE MINUTES LEFT!

AAAAA C'MON GUYS FIND IT!!

...WHAT DID HE MEAN, "ONE OF THESE THINGS IS NOT LIKE THE OTHERS"?

OKAY, UH...

HOW ABOUT PROCESS OF ELIMINATION?

LET'S SEE, WHAT REPEATING OBJECTS ARE HERE...?

...AND BENCHES...

UM... FLOOR-BOARDS?

...

LOOK LOOK

...THERE ARE FOUR OF THEM... BUT THEY ALL LOOK THE SAME...

TWO MINUTES LEFT!

NOOOOO!

IS IT EVEN HERE?!

WE'VE LOOKED EVERY-WHERE!!

....

....!

....!

ONE MINUTE THIRTY SECONDS LEFT!

....!

GRAB

LOOK!

THE FLOWERPOTS!

THEY ALL HAVE FLOWERS IN THEM...

...EXCEPT FOR THAT ONE!

FORTY-FIVE SECONDS LEFT!

THAT HAS TO BE IT!

QUICK, STAND ON THIS AND CHECK IT!

PUSH

AND THAT'S TIME!

YEAAAH!!

TEAM FIVE!

CONGRATULATIONS ON FINDING DISCOVERY CENTER'S "ARC ONE" GEOCACHE!

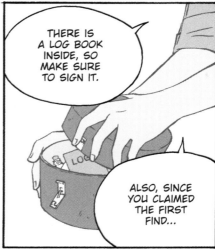
THERE IS A LOG BOOK INSIDE, SO MAKE SURE TO SIGN IT.

ALSO, SINCE YOU CLAIMED THE FIRST FIND...

...GRAB A SOUVENIR.

SCATTER

LOG

...I THINK THIS EAGLE-EYED DUO SHOULD HAVE THE FIRST PICK.

!

CHATTER

CHATTER

...THIS IS SUCH A COOL COMPASS...

DO YOU THINK IT'S ANTIQUE?

I DUNNO...

BUT I CAN USE IT WHEN I GO LOOK FOR MORE GEOCACHES.

THERE'RE MORE?! AROUND HERE?

OH YEAH, THIS TOWN HAS A WHOLE BUNCH!

MY DAD AND I GO GEOCACHING A LOT! WE EVEN HID A COUPLE.

OHHHHH, I WANNA G—

PEPPI!!

PEPPI!!!

DID YOU GUYS FIND YOUR GEOCACHE?!

YEAH, WE WERE THE FIRST ONES!

I GOT A COOL GEOCOIN, AND JAIME GOT AN AWESOME...

HEY, GUYS!

HEY, GUYS!

...

LOOK WHAT I GOT, LOOK WHAT I GOOOOT!

OOOH, NICE!

OKAY, EVERYONE ON THE BUS! TIME TO GO!

CHAPTER 3

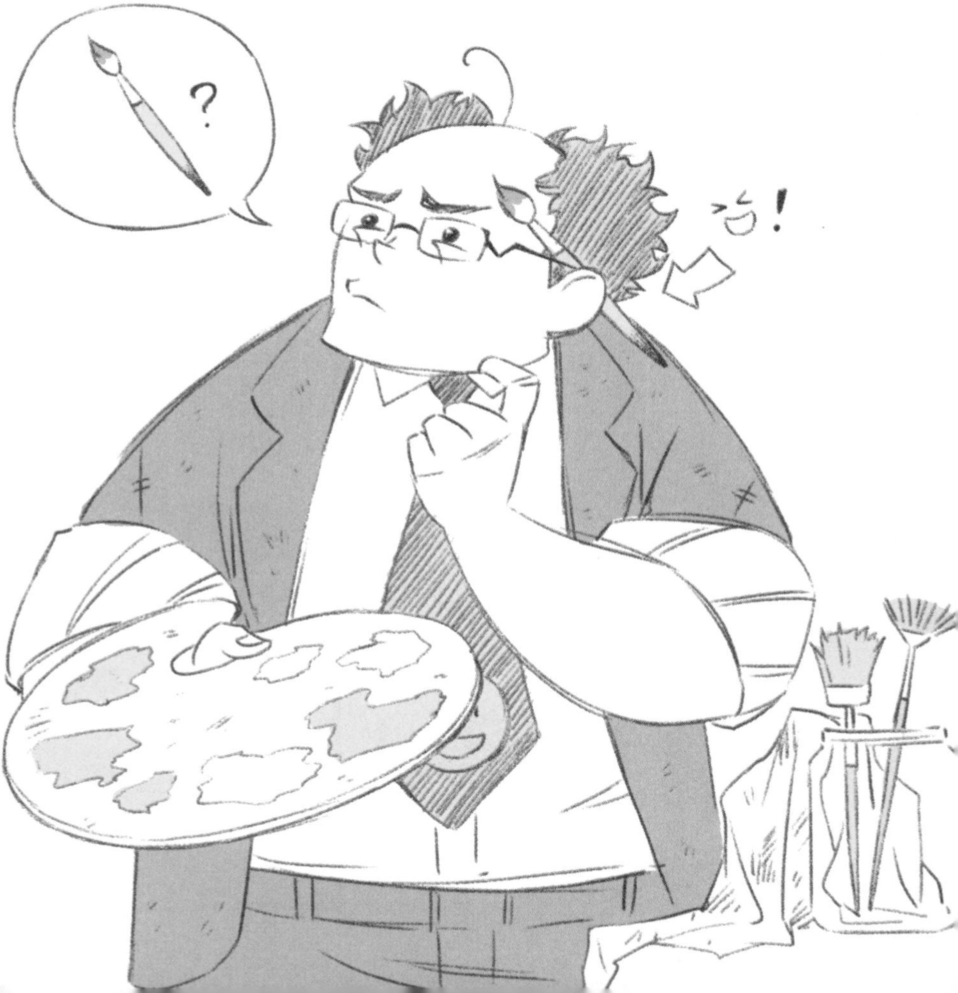

THE NEXT DAY.

...I REALLY NEED TO APOLOGIZE.

JUST GO UP AND SAY—

"I'M SORRY I PUSHED YOU."

. . .

...CAN WE BE FRIENDS?

...WE ROCKED THAT GEOCACHE HUNT.

MAYBE I SHOULD MAKE MY COMIC ABOUT THAT.

WAIT, WHAT DO YOU MEAN YOU'RE STILL *THINKING* ABOUT YOUR COMICS?!!

DID ANYONE ACTUALLY *DRAW* ONE?!!

...

ER... NOPE.

...I HAD EXTRA CHOIR PRACTICE...

...HEY, I HAD, LIKE, A HUNDRED TESTS THIS WEEK! I DIDN'T HAVE TIME!

...WE HAVE FAMILY VISITING...

NOOOOO! GUYS!!

OUR DEADLINE IS COMING UP!

MINE'S FINISHED!!

REALLY?!

...WAIT. IS IT ABOUT SUNSPOTS?

...

MAYBE?

ARE THEY SCHOOL RELATED SUNSPOTS?

...

...NO.

GUYS, REMEMBER, THESE HAVE TO BE SCHOOL RELATED COMICS! SHOW OF HANDS — WHO'S HAVING TROUBLE WITH IDEAS?

. . . .

OH.

WOW.

OKAY.

HMMMM.

TIC TOC TIC TOC

ART CLUB.

...I HAVE A SOLUTION!

ALREADY?

MEET JENNY, THE SCHOOL PAPER EDITOR...

...AND AKILAH, THE STAFF REPORTER!

THEY AGREED TO GIVE US SOME SCHOOL TOPIC GUIDANCE!

HELLO!

THERE ARE LOTS OF SCHOOL LIFE TOPICS THAT NEED COMMENTARY...

...LIKE PICTURE DAY DRAMA, CAFETERIA FOOD MYSTERIES, THE SCIENCE FAIR...

WE MADE A LIST FOR YOU! MR. R IS OFF MAKING COPIES NOW.

HE'S WHAT ?!?

HE NEEDS SUPERVISION...

AND IF YOU HAVE ANY TOPIC QUESTIONS, JUST E-MAIL ME!

JENNY, OVER TO YOU!

THANK YOU, AKILAH.

AS THE EDITOR, I ONLY HAVE A FEW THINGS TO ADD.

ONE: PLEASE FOLLOW THE TEMPLATE PROVIDED. IT WILL REALLY HELP US WITH THE LAYOUT.

TWO: PLEASE KEEP THINGS POSITIVE. WE DISCOURAGE MEAN HUMOR.

AND THREE—

MISS YOUR SUBMISSION DEADLINE, AND I WILL CANCEL YOUR PAGE FOREVER.

AND HAUNT YOUR NIGHTMARES. ALSO FOREVER.

sh-she's just kidding...

...i think

WOW, JENNY WAS INTENSE, HUH?

Y-YEAH. DID YOU SEE THAT DARK GLOW? IT'S LIKE SHE HAS SUPERNATURAL POWERS.

I-I GUESS WE'D BETTER NOT MISS THE DEADLINE!

DRAW DRAW

LOOK AT YOU, PEPPI, ALREADY DRAWING! WHAT'S YOUR IDEA?

WELL...

...I'M *TRYING* TO DO A COMIC ABOUT THE SCIENCE TRIP...

...BUT IT'S HARD TO GET IT ALL INTO JUST FOUR PANELS.

TITLE:

Find a bicycle in 45 minutes!

1. SOLVE ALL THE PUZZLES!

RUN RUN

this place was the size of texas aaaaa

TIC TAC TOE

NO NO NO

TITL

NOD NOD

NNGH

YEAH. WHO KNEW COMICS WERE SO MUCH **WOOORK**...

I STILL NEED TO PICK MY IDEA TOO. WHAT'S TAKING MR. R SO LONG?

EVERYONE! HERE ARE THE PHOTO-COPIES!!

!

h-how many?

TWENTY COPIES, JUST LIKE YOU ASKED!

!!

PREEN

PREEN

IT...IT IS TWENTY! WOW!

...WAIT. DID YOU JUST PUT THE REST IN THE RECYCLING?

...S-SOOO! DOES ANYONE HAVE ANY CARTOONING QUESTIONS? I GOT HOW-TO BOOKS FROM THE LIBRARY!

OH, MR. R...

HEE HEE

SAY WHAT YOU WANT ABOUT THE ART CLUB, BUT I LOVE IT HERE.

YES, WE SPIN OUR WHEELS A LOT AND DON'T GET MUCH DONE.

WHAT CAN I SAY? WE'RE EASILY DISTRACTED.

BUT IT'S AMAZING JUST TO BE HERE WITH OTHER ARTISTS, TRYING THINGS.

I WONDER IF THAT'S WHAT THE SCIENCE CLUB IS LIKE FOR JAIME?

BANG

WHAT!! WHAT WAS THAT!!

...WHAT?

WHAT ARE YOU DOING OUT HERE?!

ARE YOU LAUNCHING ROCKETS INTO LOCKERS?

YOU'LL DAMAGE SCHOOL PROPERTY!!

KTK

WE ARE COLLECTING VELOCITY DATA FOR OUR SCIENCE FAIR PROJECT.

WHAT IS THIS.

W-WE'RE COLLECTING VELOCITY DATA...

MR LEE, WHAT HAVE I SAID ABOUT SETTING UP UNSAFE EXPERIMENTS IN MY ABSENCE?

...

...not to...?

PACK THIS UP IMMEDIATELY, OR I WILL TAKE YOU OFF THE FAIR TEAM.

WOOOAH

...

HMPF.

AFTER SCHOOL.

...WOW. THE SCIENCE CLUB'S GOTTEN CHEEKY LATELY!

IF MISS TOBINS TOLD ME NOT TO DO SOMETHING...

...I WOULD NOT DO IT. BECAUSE I WOULD CHOOSE LIFE!

I KNOW, RIGHT?

I CAN'T BELIEVE THOSE JERKS ARE GETTING A TABLE AND WE AREN'T. WHAT HAVE THEY EVER DONE FOR THE SCHOOL?

...

...BESIDES WINNING ALL THE REGIONAL SCIENCE FAIR AWARDS AND MAKING THE SCHOOL LOOK GOOD...?

...YEAH, BESIDES THAT...

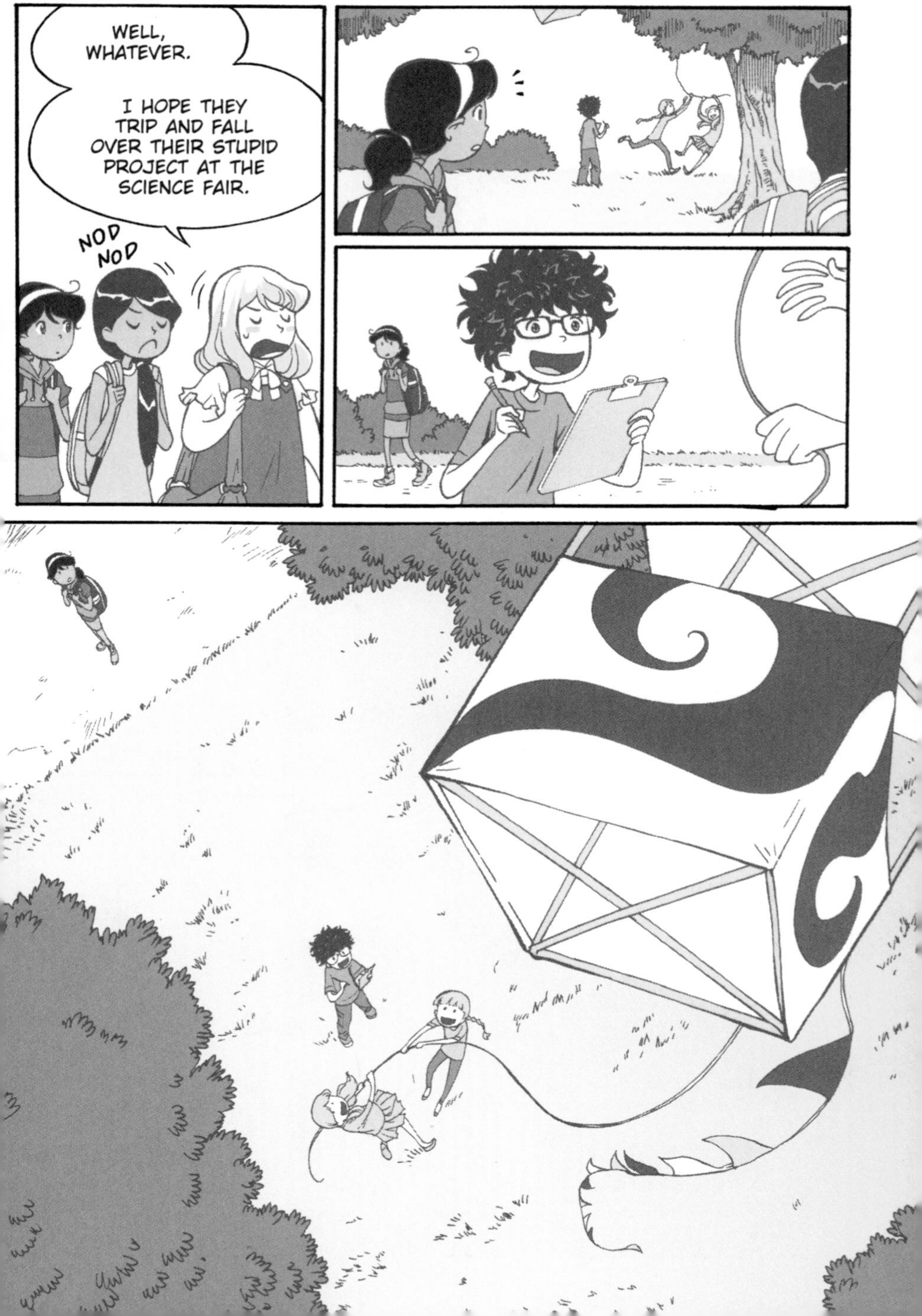
WELL, WHATEVER.
I HOPE THEY TRIP AND FALL OVER THEIR STUPID PROJECT AT THE SCIENCE FAIR.
NOD NOD

...

...S-SO, UM...

YOU GUYS HAVE BEEN FLYING A LOT OF THINGS LATELY. IS THAT FOR THE SCIENCE FAIR?

...YEAH. THEY'RE PRESENTING A PROJECT ON AERODYNAMICS.

..."THEY"? YOU'RE NOT PART OF THE FAIR TEAM?

...

I WAS.

BUT I ASKED MISS TOBINS TO TAKE ME OFF.

OH!

HOW COME?

...

...I DON'T REALLY LIKE COMPETITIONS.

I JUST WANT TO DO THE SCIENCE STUFF.

I NEED TO GET BACK THERE AND HELP THEM PREPARE. DO YOU HAVE ANY MORE HOMEWORK QUESTIONS?

OH... UM...

PACK PACK

NO, I THINK I UNDERSTAND THE REST. THANK YOU!

WHOOPS

FLUTTER

FLUTTER

I GOT THEM.

...HEY, IS THIS...?

....!

TITLE:

Find a geocache in 45 minutes!

TIC TOC

NO NO NO NO

TITLE:

1. SOLVE ALL THE PUZZLES!

RUN RUN

this museum is the size of Texas aaaaaa

2. USE COORDINATES TO FIND LOCATION.

3. ONE OF THE THINGS IS THE OTHER

I-I'M TRYING TO DO A COMIC ABOUT OUR SCIENCE TRIP! WITH THE GEOCACHE?

READ

SHF

BYE.

AAAAAAAAA

...IIIIT'S MORNING ANNOUNCEMENTS AGAIN! WE'LL START WITH A BIG "GOOD LUCK!!" TO OUR SCIENCE CLUB AT THE REGIONAL SCIENCE FAIR THIS WEEKEND!

BERRYBROOK MIDDLE SCHOOL

LATE LATE LATE

RRRRING

MISS TORRES...

A!

...*EXCELLENT* JOB ON YOUR TEST. I KNEW YOU HAD IT IN YOU!

THANK YOU.

YOU'VE SHOWN *REMARKABLE* IMPROVEMENT. I'D LIKE TO SEE YOU CONTINUE ON YOUR OWN.

SO LET'S SUSPEND THE TUTORING SESSIONS.

....!

I THINK YOU'LL DO FINE NOW. AND JAIME NEEDS TO FOCUS ON THE SCIENCE FAIR PREP, ANYWAY.

...OH.

OKAY.

GOOD LUCK, PENELOPE!

...

...WELL, I GUESS THIS'LL MAKE IT EASIER FOR ME TO AVOID HIM.

...RIGHT?

ART CLUB.

GUYS, GUESS WHAT! I FINISHED MY COMIC!

WHAT?

OHHH, HEE-HEE...

TITLE: Bad Picture Day

BAD HAIR ON PICTURE DAY?! TRY THESE SOLUTIONS!!!

STYLISH HAT!

#1

TEAM SPIRIT!

AVOIDANCE

mom: think i have a fever

by Maribella Samson

HA HA!

...HEY, IT'S PRETTY FUNNY.

...HOW ARE YOU ALREADY DONE?!

WHO ELSE IS DONE?!

ANYONE **ABOUT** TO BE DONE?

...ANYONE NEED HELP?

...

NNGH

...I NEED A SOLUTION FOR THE "I'M STILL ON THE FIRST PANEL OF MY COMIC" PROBLEM...

PEPPI, HOW'S YOURS GOING?

A-ALMOST DONE WITH THE ROUGH?

COME ON, EVERYONE! WE CAN DO THIS!

FIGHT! WIN!

WHINE

MONDAY.

BERRYBROOK MIDDLE SCHOOL

...YOUR MOOOOOONDAY MORNING ANNOUNCEMENTS!

GUYS, DID YOU SEE THIS?

SLAM

REGIONAL SCIENCE FAIR FOULED BY PRANK GONE TOO FAR!

MY DAD WAS READING THE NEWSPAPER THIS MORNING, AND I WAS, LIKE, HEEEEEY, THOSE GUYS LOOK FAMILIAR...

HEY, THAT'S OUR SCIENCE CLUB!

WHAT DID THEY DOOO...?

THEY PULLED A PRANK AND *RUINED* THE SCIENCE FAIR THIS WEEKEND!

I THINK THEY SET OFF THE EMERGENCY SPRINKLERS OR SOMETHING...

MAN, MISS TOBINS IS GONNA BE PIIIISSED...

RRUUMB!

SCRBBL
SCRBBL

SCIENCE CLASS.

...WOW.

I ALMOST FEEL SORRY FOR THE SCIENCE CLUB.

RRING

SCIENCE ROOM

BLEEAH

...ALMOST.

...DO YOU THINK SHE'LL FEED THEM TO THE VENUS FLYTRAP NOW OR AFTER SHE YELLS AT THEM?

AFTER, OF COURSE. THEY'LL BE EASIER TO DIGEST ONCE SHE CHEWS THEM OUT.

HA!

GUYS, GUYS!! MR. R!!

WHOA, YOU OKAY? WHAT HAPPENED?!

I WAS JUST...

...TALKING TO THE PRINCIPAL...

...SAYING HOW...

...HOW WE'RE WORKING HARD ON OUR COMICS...

...AND THAT...

HUFF

HUFF HUFF

TEN MINUTES AGO.

...IF THE DELINQUENTS FROM THE SCIENCE CLUB WILL HAVE A TABLE AT THE FAIR, THEN SO SHOULD THE ART CLUB!

PRINCIP

...

SH FFF

...!

MISS SAMSON, I HAVE SOMETHING TO SAY TO BOTH YOUR CLUBS.

PLEASE MAKE SURE THEY ARE LISTENING TO THE P.A. SPEAKER IN THEIR CLUB ROOMS IN FIFTEEN MINUTES.

PRESENT TIME.

...

...

ART CLUB.

SCIENCE CLUB.

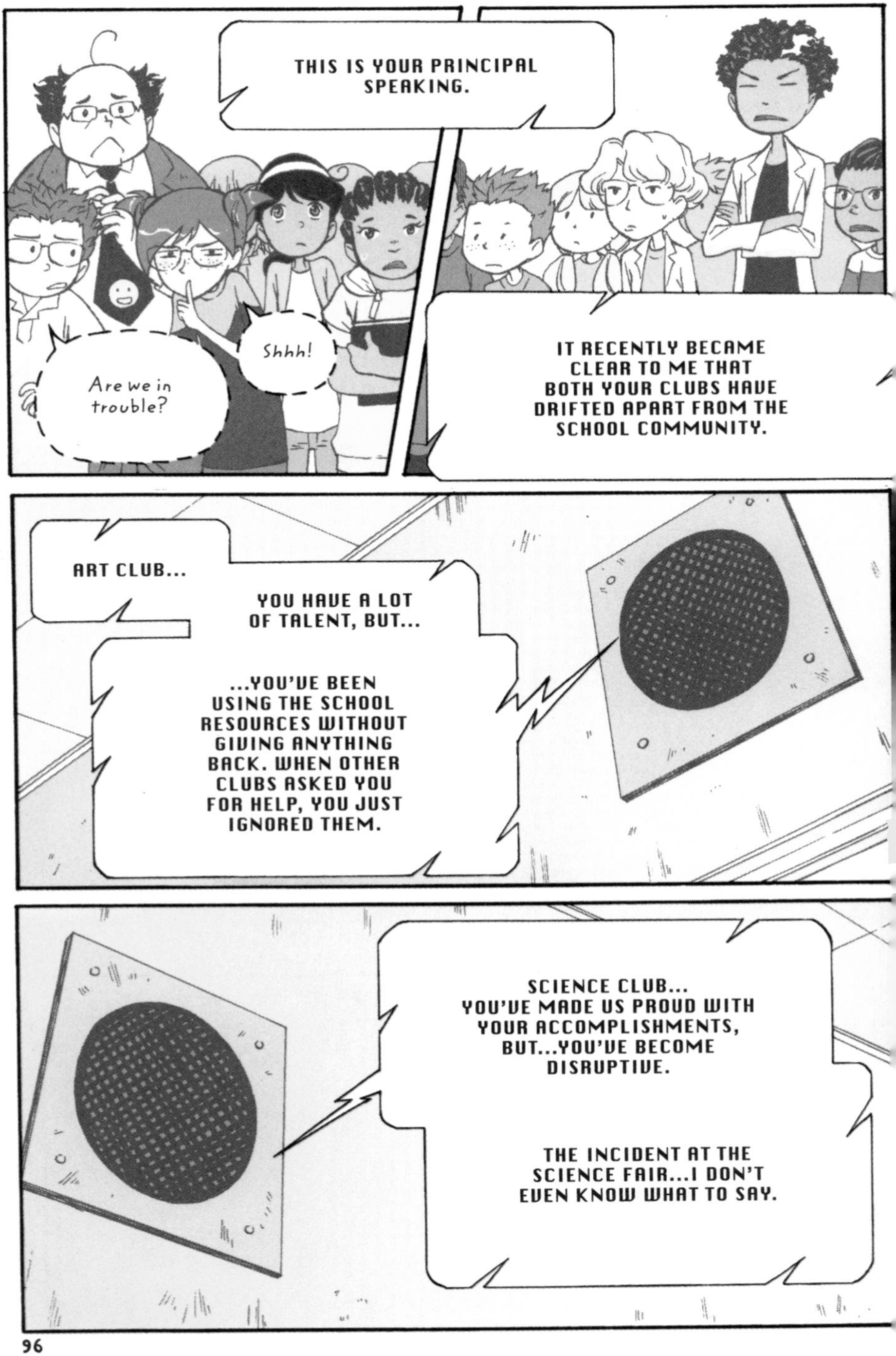

THIS IS YOUR PRINCIPAL SPEAKING.
Are we in trouble?
Shhh!
IT RECENTLY BECAME CLEAR TO ME THAT BOTH YOUR CLUBS HAVE DRIFTED APART FROM THE SCHOOL COMMUNITY.
ART CLUB...
YOU HAVE A LOT OF TALENT, BUT...
...YOU'VE BEEN USING THE SCHOOL RESOURCES WITHOUT GIVING ANYTHING BACK. WHEN OTHER CLUBS ASKED YOU FOR HELP, YOU JUST IGNORED THEM.
SCIENCE CLUB... YOU'VE MADE US PROUD WITH YOUR ACCOMPLISHMENTS, BUT...YOU'VE BECOME DISRUPTIVE.
THE INCIDENT AT THE SCIENCE FAIR...I DON'T EVEN KNOW WHAT TO SAY.

I *KNOW* THAT BOTH YOUR CLUBS ARE BETTER THAN THAT.

SO HERE IS MY CHALLENGE TO YOU.

IN THE NEXT TWO MONTHS, UNDERTAKE AND COMPLETE PROJECTS THAT CONTRIBUTE TO THE SCHOOL COMMUNITY.

YOUR PROJECTS WILL THEN BE VOTED ON BY THE SCHOOL.

AND THE CLUB WHOSE PROJECT IS VOTED MOST SUCCESSFUL...

...WILL GET THE TABLE AT THE SCHOOL CLUB FAIR.

THE OTHER CLUB WILL THINK HARD ON HOW THEY COULD DO BETTER NEXT YEAR.

GOOD LUCK!

I'LL BE WATCHING.

CLICK

OKAY, IT'S OFFICIALLY **ON** PEOPLE!

NOD NOD

WE HAVE TO MAKE "COMIC PUNCH" *AMAZING!*

WE CANNOT LET THE SCIENCE CLUB WIN THIS!!

HEY, ART CLUB.

KEEP *DREAMING.*

THAT TABLE IS *OURS,* AND OURS IT'LL *STAY.*

HEY, SCIENCE CLUB.

WE'RE GOING TO MOP THE FLOOR WITH YOU. I HOPE YOU'RE READY.

UGH. THEY ARE *SO* GOING DOWN.

PEPPI! WE NEED TO HAVE AN EDITORIAL MEETING!

COME OVER TO MY HOUSE TOMORROW?

U-UH.

S-SURE?

THE NEXT DAY.

HUFF HUFF

...ACTUALLY, I HAD OTHER PLANS FOR TODAY.

...WHY AM I SUCH A PUSHOVER?

I WISH I HAD MARIBELLA'S MAGICAL GO-GETTING CONFIDENCE POWERS...

PEPPI, THERE YOU ARE!

...!

WOW.

...THIS HOUSE IS *HUGE*!

PARENTAL UNITS ARE STILL AT WORK, SO WE HAVE THE HOUSE TO OURSELVES.

C'MON, MY DAD SAID WE CAN USE HIS OFFICE. IT'S THIS WAY!

HE'S GOT A FULL SCANNER/PRINTER SETUP, SO WE WON'T HAVE TO RELY ON SCHOOL EQUIPMENT.

...!

PLOP

SO YOU READY TO ROCK THIS?!

ROLL

UH.

I'M...AFRAID TO TOUCH ANYTHING.

...YOUR DAD'S OFFICE IS AMAZING.

WELL, MY *DAD* IS AMAZING.

LOOK! THERE'S HIM SHAKING HANDS WITH THE *MAYOR!*

AND HE'S GOT AN MBA BECAUSE HE'S REALLY SMART...

...AND HE DOES BOXING BECAUSE HE'S—

VRRRM

....!

SLAM

THAT'S HIM!

HE'S HOME! EARLY...

UH...

QUICK!

LOOK BUSY!

MARIBELLA?

HI, DAD! WELCOME HOME!

THIS IS PENELOPE. I TOLD YOU ABOUT HER YESTERDAY?

OF COURSE, OF COURSE!

HELLO, PENELOPE, GOOD TO MEETCHA!

YOU GIRLS ARE ALREADY WORKING? THAT'S WHAT I LIKE TO SEE!

I WAS SHOWING PENELOPE YOUR SCANNER SETUP. THANKS FOR LETTING US USE IT!

PAT PAT

HA-HA! ALL THE BEST TOOLS FOR MY LITTLE CHAMPION.

YER GONNA CRUSH 'EM, RIGHT?!

YEAH!

FIGHT!

WIN!

PUT LOSERS IN THE TRASH BIN!

...!

AHHH, I'M SO GLAD YOU TAKE AFTER ME AND NOT YOUR LAZY BXXXX MOTHER.

...

ALL RIGHT, I'LL LET YOU GIRLS WORK!

DON'T DISAPPOINT ME.

SLAM

WE **HAVE** TO WIN THIS.

LET'S WORK HARD.

. . .

WOW.

I'VE NEVER SEEN MARIBELLA LIKE THAT.

IT'S LIKE SHE'S AFRAID OF HER OWN *DAD*!

...THOUGH HER DAD IS PRETTY SCARY...

BR R

...AND HE CALLED HER MOM A BAD WORD. THAT'S NOT COO —

HOOOONK

SWERVE

!!!
...

HHUH
HHUH

UH...
UH...

...OKAY, NEW GOAL IN LIFE—*DON'T GET RUN OVER BY A CAR!*

OH MY GOSH, ARE YOU OKAY?!

?—

...JAIME!

ALL RIGHT, I CALLED YOUR MOTHER, AND SHE'LL BE HERE TO GET YOU IN ABOUT AN HOUR.

Awkward *adj.*
2. ...*THIS.*

O-OKAY.

I'M SO GLAD YOU COULD COME VISIT!

I DON'T OFTEN GET TO MEET JAIME'S FRIENDS. ARE YOU FROM HIS SCIENCE CLUB?

U-UH.

N-NO...

....!

NO, MOM. SHE'S FROM THE ART CLUB.

SHE'S REALLY GOOD.

OH! YOU'RE AN ARTIST? SO AM I! WHAT DO YOU LIKE TO DRAW?

U-UH, WELL...

....!

MERMAIDS.

OH, UM!

OTHER THINGS TOO! LIKE HORSES, AND... I DREW MY BUNNY, PEPPER.

YOU HAVE A BUNNY? HOW WONDERFUL!

I JUST FINISHED A COMMISSION FOR A BUNNY PORTRAIT.

JAIME, COULD YOU GO GET THAT FROM MY STUDIO?

OKAY.

AND THE STUDIES SKETCHBOOK.

...

...

...WHY'S SHE SUDDENLY SO QUIET...?

...ARE YOU THE GIRL WHO PUSHED HIM?

...

...

Y-yes.

I-I'm really sorry.

PEEK

...

YOU SHOULD TELL HIM THAT SOMETIME.

CLATTER

ARGH!

OKAY, J?

YOU HAVE, LIKE, A METRIC TON OF SKETCHBOOKS IN THERE. I DIDN'T KNOW WHICH ONE.

HA-HA, WELL, I'LL FIND THE RIGHT ONE.

DRAWING

FWUMP

IN THE MEANTIME, WHY DON'T YOU SHOW PENELOPE YOUR DAD'S WORKSHOP AND WHAT YOU TINKERERS HAVE BEEN BUILDING?

OH, YEAH! WANNA SEE THE GEOCACHE WE'RE GOING TO HIDE?!

Y-YEAH!

THIS WAY!

FLIP FLIP

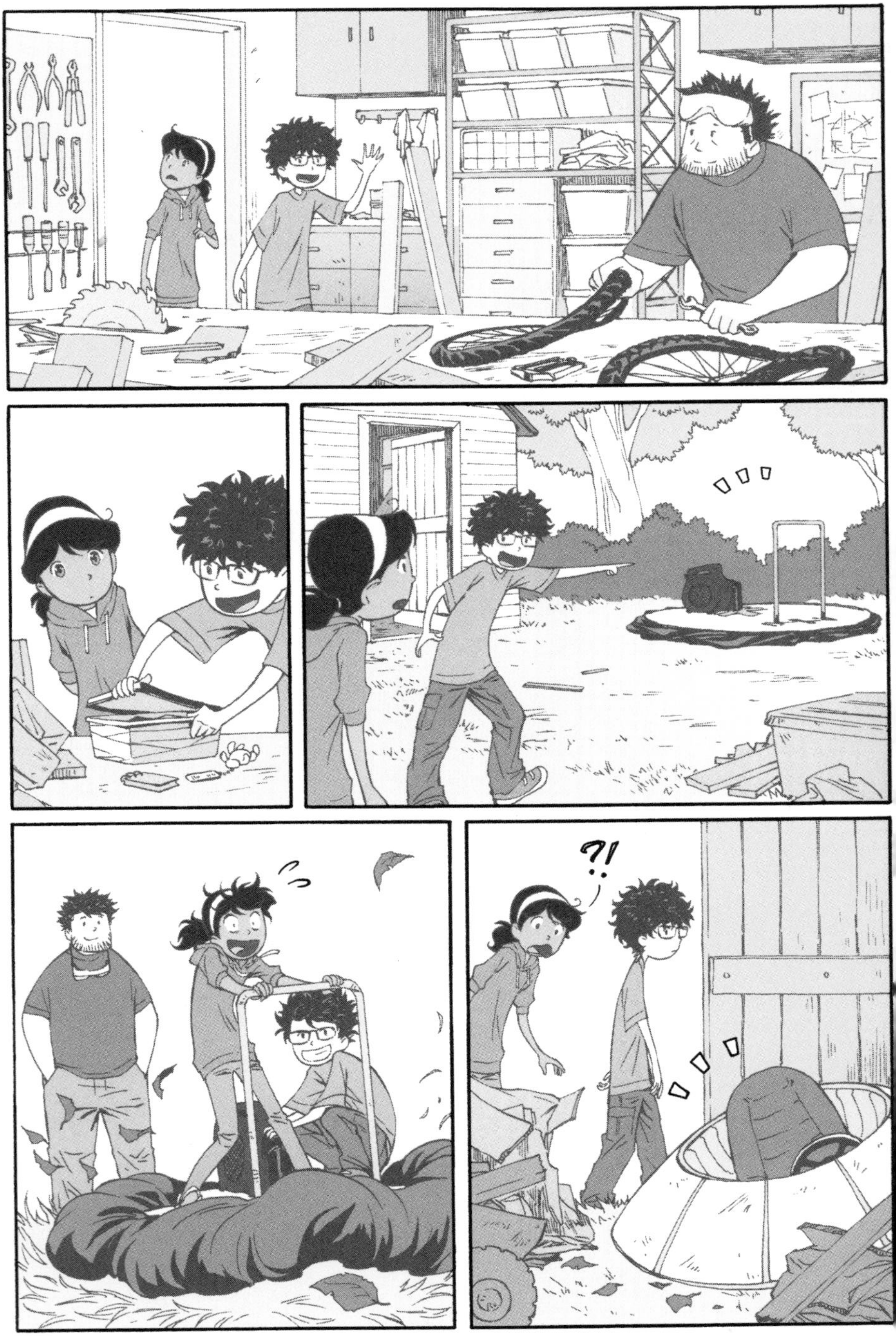
?!

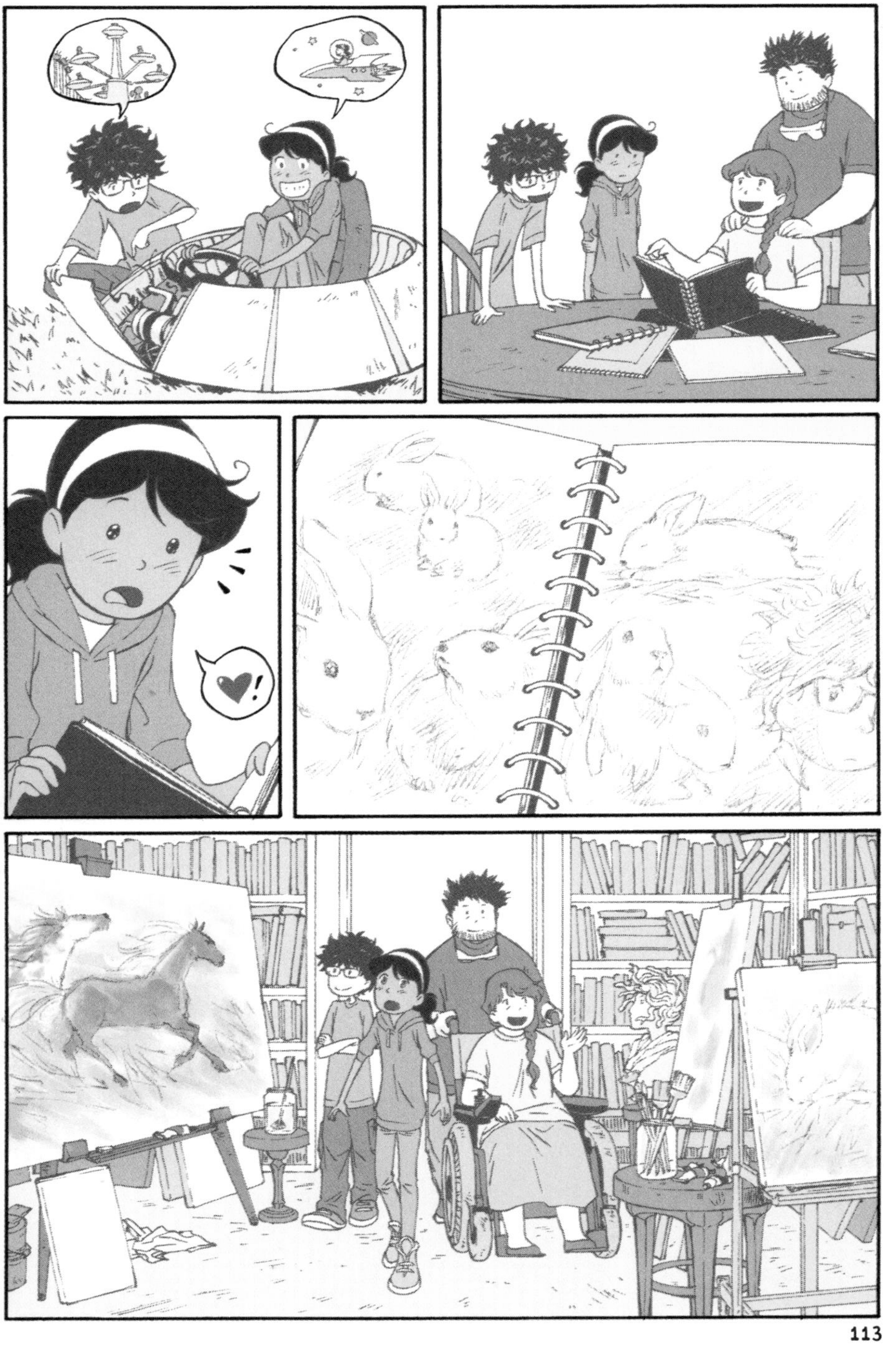
♥!

. . .

...I DON'T WANT TO LEAVE.

PEPPI! ♥

HELLO HELLO

...I COULD'VE WALKED. WE'RE JUST TWO STREETS OVER FROM YOU!

. . .

OH! COME FOR DINNER SOMETIME, THEN! I INSIST!

...I CAN'T BELIEVE HE WAS ALREADY FIXING YOUR BIKE!

THAT'S REAL GOOD PEOPLE, HON. WE'LL HAVE TO COME BACK WITH *FOOD*.

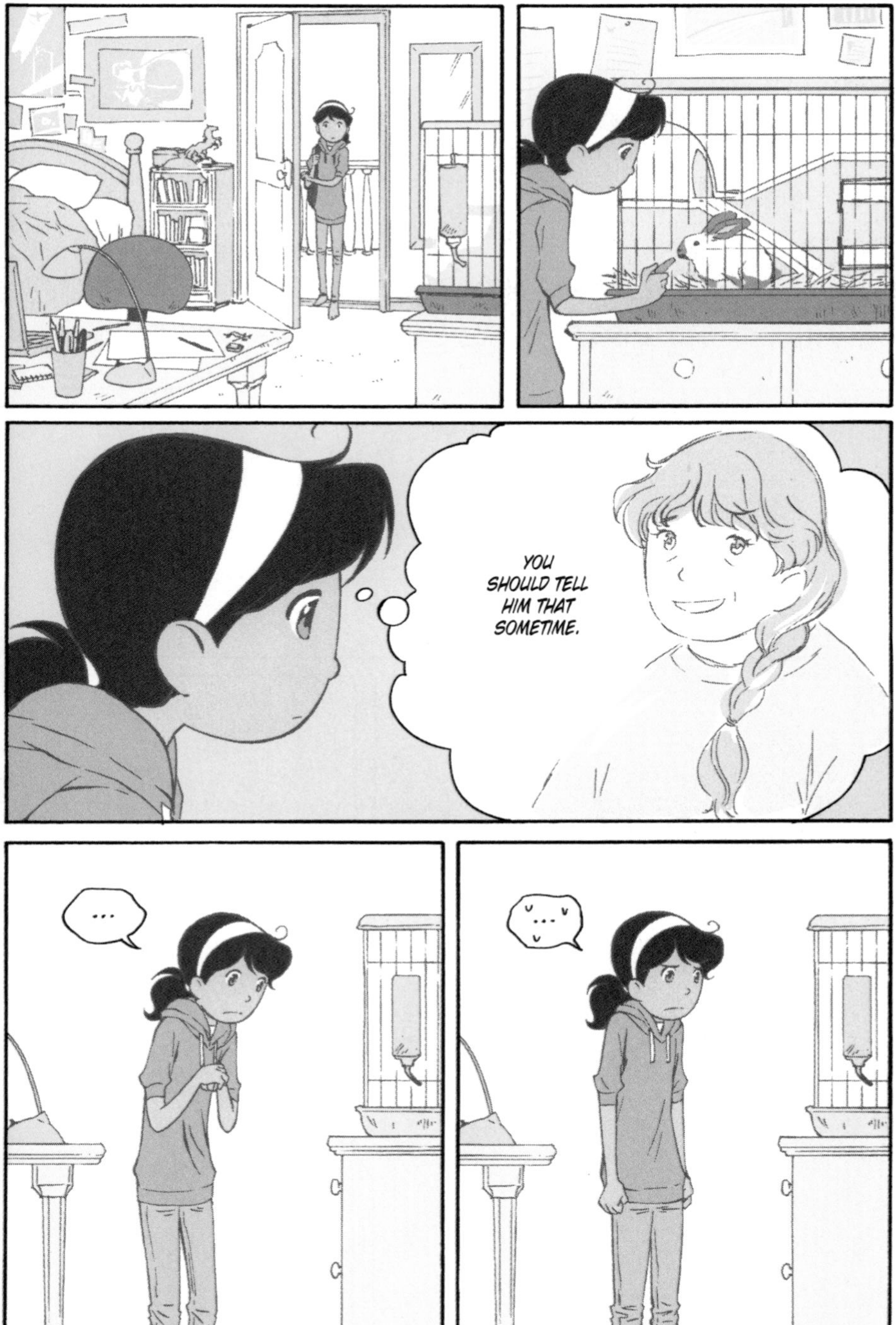
YOU SHOULD TELL HIM THAT SOMETIME.
...
...

DASH

SNATCH

SCRIBBLE

SCRIBBLE

SCRIBBLE

hi, Jaime, I should've said this a long time ago

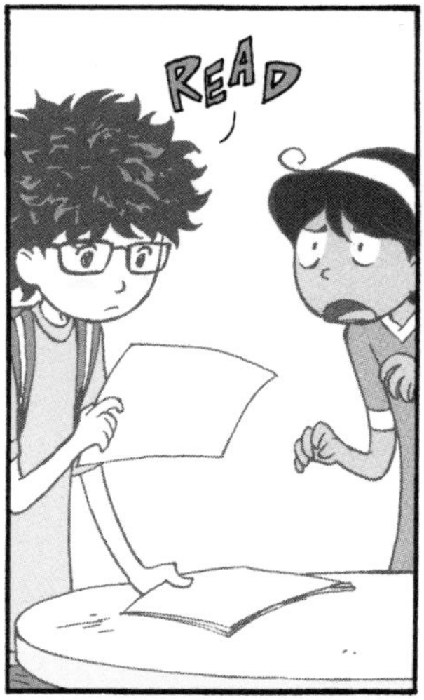
READ

CHAPTER 4

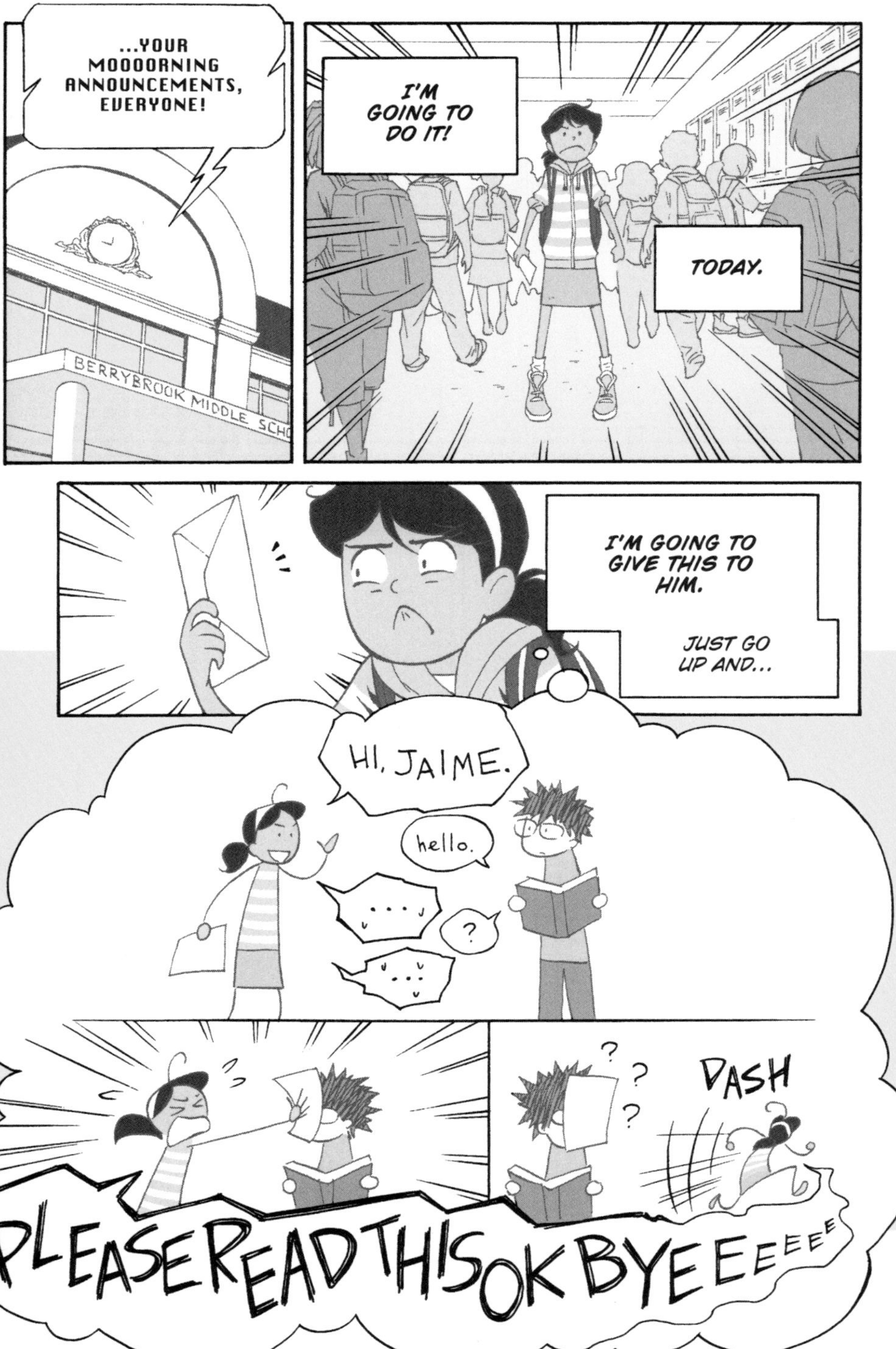
...YOUR MOOOORNING ANNOUNCEMENTS, EVERYONE!
BERRYBROOK MIDDLE SCHO
I'M GOING TO DO IT!
TODAY.
I'M GOING TO GIVE THIS TO HIM.
JUST GO UP AND...
HI, JAIME.
hello.
...
?
...
?
?
?
DASH
PLEASE READ THIS OK BYEEEEEE

. . .

THAT...DIDN'T GO WELL, EVEN IN MY *HEAD.*

...I'M JUST GONNA PUT IT IN HIS LOCKER.

YEAH, YEAH, GOOD PLAN!

...!

PEPPI*!*

SILLY GIRL, THAT'S NOT YOUR LOCKER!

DID YOU STAY UP TOO LATE AGAIN?

HA! HA!

YEAH, I WAS DRAWING...

C'MON, GUYS, BELL'S GONNA RING!

...IT'S OKAY, I'LL JUST COME BACK DURING LUNCH.

LUNCH.

PEPPI.

...!

HOW'S YOUR COMIC GOING?

UH. A-ALMOST DONE?

LIE LIE LIIIE

SHE STAYED UP LATE TO DRAW, SHE SAID!

REALLY?!

....

YOU'RE THE BESSSSST!!

WHAT ABOUT YOU, TESSA? WHATCHA DRAWING?

A DRAGON! LOOK, SHE'S—

IS SHE PART OF YOUR COMIC?

...SH-SHE CAN BE...?

SLINK SLINK SLINK

TMP TMP TMP TMP

LUNCH IS ALMOST OVER! PLEASE DON'T RING, BELL!!

ALMOST AT HIS LOCKER, ALMOST...

....!

NOOOOOOO!

...OKAY. DESPERATE TIMES CALL FOR DESPERATE MEASURES.

SCIENCE CLASS.

MISS TOBINS.

...YES?

MAY I PLEASE BE EXCUSED FOR A MINUTE?

...!

UH.

...YES.

...ARE YOU OKAY, MISS TOR—

DASH

BE RIGHT BACK.

I CAN DO THIS.

I CAN DO THIS.

I CAN DO THIS!!

122

WIGGLE
WIGGLE

SHF

SKIDD

HUH.

...I...

I DID IT.

FINALLY...

TIC
TOC
TIC
TOC

ART CLUB.

PEPPI, WHAT'S WRONG NOW?

I FEEL LIKE I'VE LIVED A THOUSAND LIFETIMES...

...AND AGED A THOUSAND YEARS...

...WAIT. THAT MATH DOESN'T ADD UP.

PLOP

NO TIME TO SLACK, GUYS! LET'S DRAW!! LET'S FINISH THESE!

OUR DEADLINE IS FRIDAY!

FELICITY, WHY ARE YOU DRAWING ELVES?? ARE YOU DONE WITH YOUR COMIC?!

I-IT'S JUST A WARM-UP!

JENSEN, THOSE BETTER NOT BE SUNSPOTS I'M LOOKING AT!

WHAT?! NO! IT'S THE PRINCIPAL!

...OH. UH.

I-IT LOOKS JUST LIKE HIM! KEEP GOING!

one... more... panel...

...

MARIBELLAAA! I CAN'T FIT ALL OF THIS INTO JUST FOUR PANELS! I NEED A PAGE!

HEY, ART CLUB.

HOW'S YOUR AMAZING COMIC PROJECT GOING?

YOU GIVING UP YET?

IT'S GOING JUST *FINE*, FOR YOUR FAT INFORMATION.

WHAT ABOUT *YOU*? DID YOU BLOW A HOLE IN A WALL SOMEWHERE YET?

NOD NOD

OH, NO WALL DAMAGE THIS TIME...BUT WE'VE GOT SOMETHING THAT'LL BLOW *YOUR* STUPID CARTOONS RIGHT OUT OF THIS COMPETITION.

OH YEAH? AND WHAT'S *THAT*?

WOULDN'T *YOU* LIKE TO KNOW.

...

LATER, LOSERS!

NO, SERIOUSLY, WHAT IS IT...?

WEEEEE NEED TO FIND OUT WHAT THEY'RE MAKING.

PFFT, THEY'RE PROBABLY JUST BLUFFING.

...PROBABLY...

125

...MAN, I NEED AT LEAST HALF A PAGE! MY STORY'S **LONG!**

MINE TOO...

WELL, WE ONLY HAVE ONE PAGE IN THE PAPER FOR **EVERY**ONE...

YOU'RE THE CO-EDITOR. CAN'T YOU MAKE MARIBELLA GET US MORE SPACE...?

UH...

PENELOPE?

GULP!

HEY, ISN'T HE FROM THE SCIENCE CLUB?

HEY, IF YOU'RE HERE TO HARASS HER, YOU CAN FORGET—

YOU SURE?

WELL, OKAY...

NO, NO, NO, HE'S GOOD, IT'S OKAY! THAT'S MY SCIENCE TUTOR!

YOU GUYS GO AHEAD. I'LL SEE YOU TOMORROW!

I GOT YOUR LETTER

DO YOU HATE ME?!!

....!

HATE...?

WHA...? ...NO...

BUT I PUSHED YOU!! IN FRONT OF THE WHOLE SCHOOL!

I'M SO SORRY.

...OH.

YEAH, THAT...

. . .

. . .

...MY MOM SAYS...THERE ARE BAD PEOPLE WHO HURT OTHERS FOR FUN...

...AND THERE ARE GOOD PEOPLE WHO DO IT BY ACCIDENT. LIKE, THEY MAKE A MISTAKE?

...I THINK YOU'RE A GOOD PERSON.

YOU JUST MADE A MISTAKE.

. . .

...I DON'T EVEN KNOW WHAT TO SAY...

HA HA

...AND THIS IS REALLY—

HEY, LOOK! IT'S NERDER! AND HIS GIRLFRIEND!

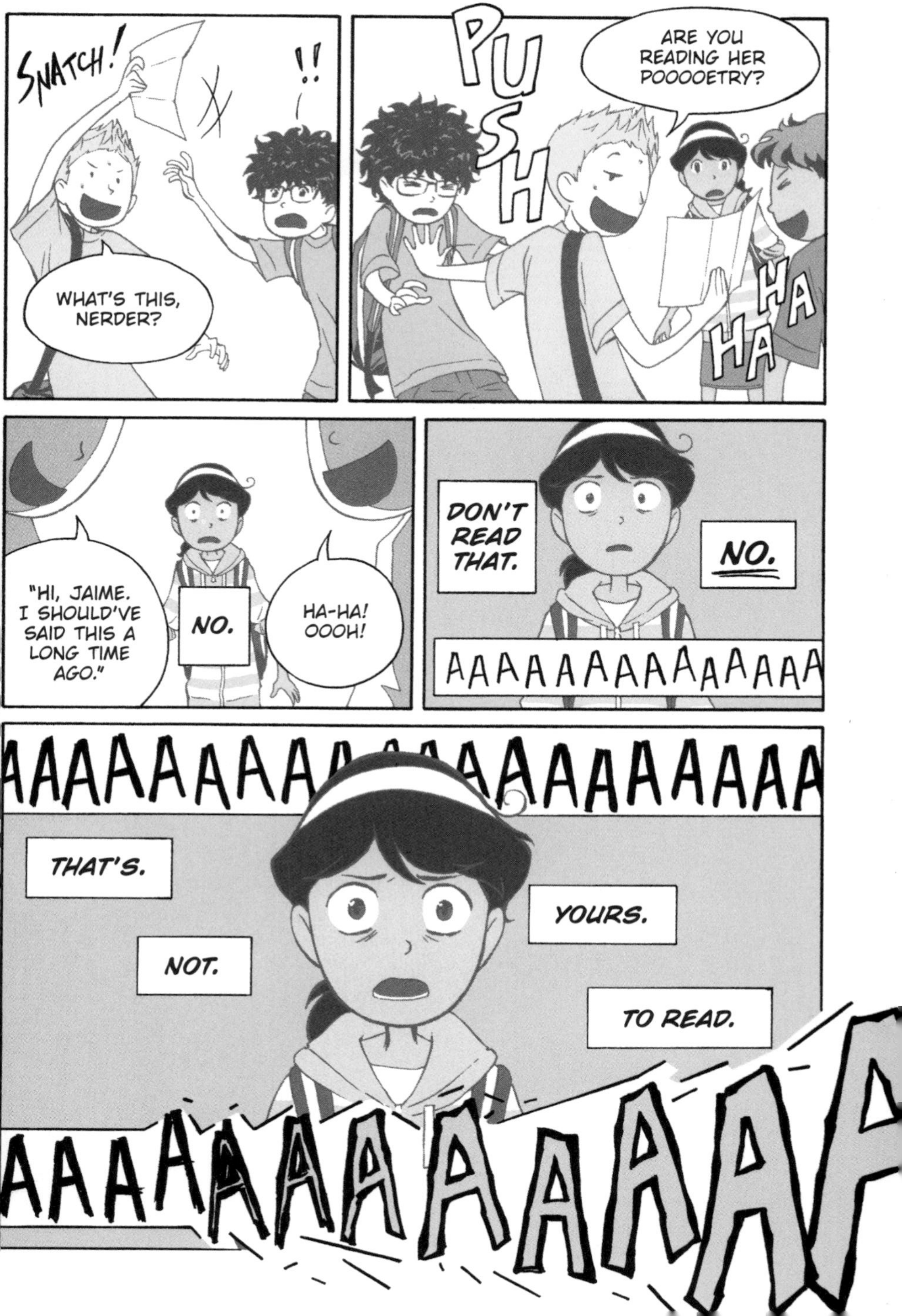

SNATCH!
!!
WHAT'S THIS, NERDER?
PUSH
ARE YOU READING HER POOOOETRY?
HA HA HA
"HI, JAIME. I SHOULD'VE SAID THIS A LONG TIME AGO."
NO.
HA-HA! OOOH!
DON'T READ THAT.
NO.
AAAAAAAAAAAAA
AAAAAAAAAAAAAAAAAAA
THAT'S.
NOT.
YOURS.
TO READ.
AAAAAAAAAAAAA

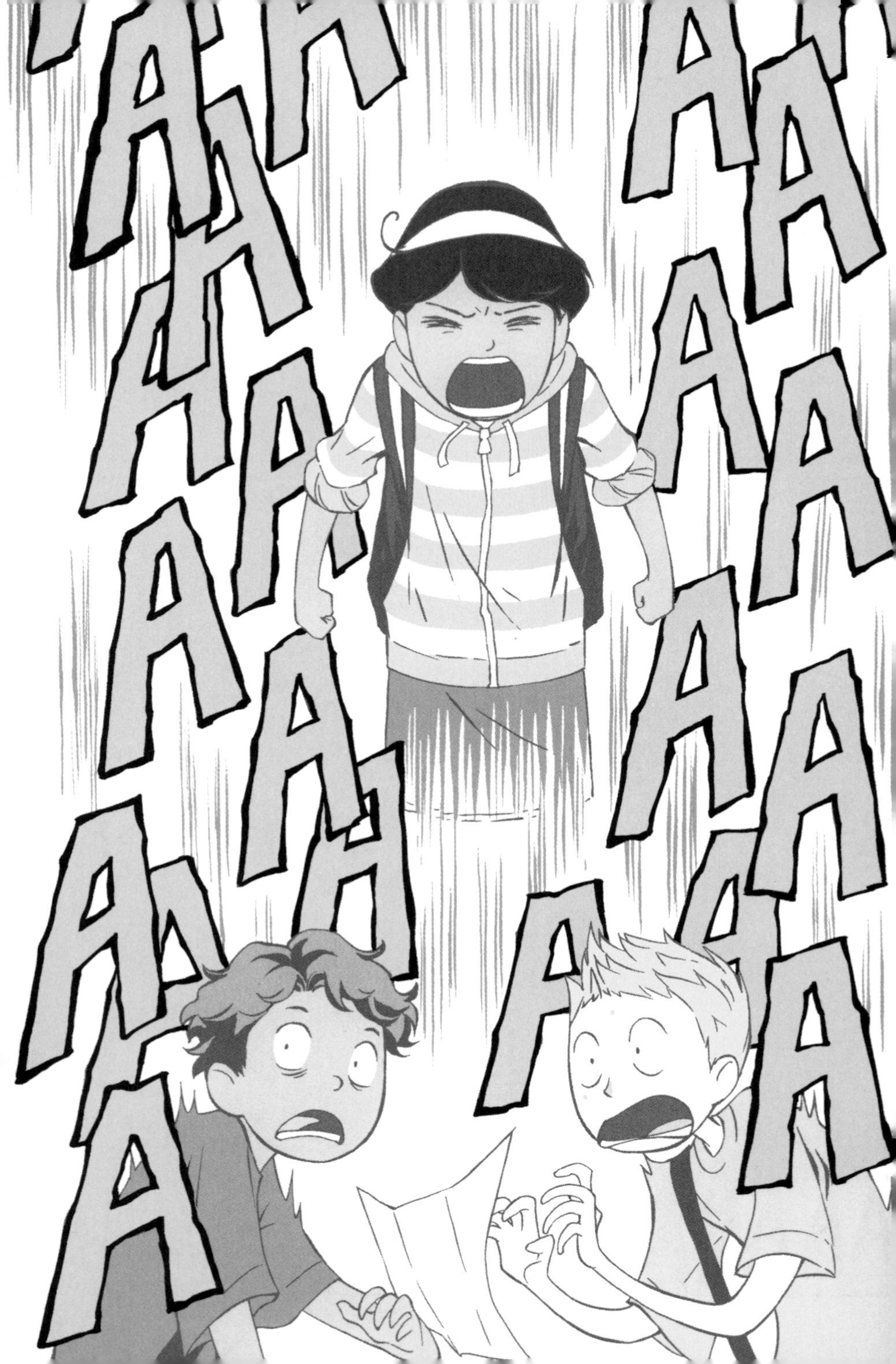

SH-SHUT UP! ARE YOU CRAZY?!

...A TEACHER'S GONNA HEAR!

LET'S GET OUT OF HERE!!

I HEARD A SCREAM!! WHO WAS THAT?!

WHAT HAPPENED?!

FOSTER! YANIC! WHAT...

HHUH HHUH HUH

PENELOPE!!

ARE YOU TWO OKAY?!

131

...I'VE NEVER SCREAMED LIKE THAT BEFORE IN MY *LIFE*. WOW.

...MY THROAT KINDA HURTS.

THAT *WAS* A PRETTY AMAZING SCREAM.

DO YOU THINK EVERYONE IN TOWN HEARD ME?

HA HA HA

I THINK EVERYONE IN *SPACE* HEARD YOU.

THAT WAS *AWESOME* VOCAL PROJECTION.

...

THOSE TWO ARE BULLIES.

YEAH...

IT'S *NOT* OKAY TO BULLY. DIDN'T ANYONE TELL THEM?

IT'S *MEAN*. AND *WRONG*.

... YEAH.

...HEH.

THEY ACT TOUGH, BUT...DID YOU SEE THEIR FACES? WHEN THEY REALIZED A TEACHER MIGHT COME?

I'VE **NEVER** SEEN THEM RUN THAT FAST.

I THOUGHT THEY'D BREAK THE DOOR.

HA HA!

LIKE A CARTOON!

...OR, HEY! A COMIC STRIP!

HA-HA, YEAH!

AND THE LAST PANEL IS JUST THEIR BODY-SHAPED HOLES IN A WALL!

HAHAHA. YESSS.

...

SO, UM...

YOU LIKE COMICS TOO, HUH?

...THIS TURNED OUT TO BE A GOOD DAY AFTER ALL.

BYE!

BYE!

I FINALLY SAID I WAS SORRY.

...AND I THINK I MADE A FRIEND.

RRING

CHIRP CHIRP

BERRYBROOK M...

IIIIIIT'S THURSDAY MORNING, EVERYONE! YOU KNOW WHAT THAT MEANS!

IT MEANS I'M **DEAD, SO DEAD!** THERE'S NO WAY I'LL BE DONE WITH MY COMIC TODAY!

ME NEITHER...

WELL, WE STILL HAVE LUNCH!

AND UNTIL THE END OF ART CLUB TODAY!

NNNNGH!

PEPPI!

YOU'LL COME TO MY PLACE TONIGHT TO HELP SCAN AND EDIT, RIGHT?!

OH!

UH, YES!

LUNCH.

MUNCH

SCRIBBLE MUNCH

SCRIBBLE

MY MATH TEACHER TOOK MY COMIC.

WHAT?!!

I-I WAS TRYING TO DRAW SOME OF IT IN MATH, BUT HE SAW AND—

ARGH! WE NEED THAT BACK! LET'S GO!

SCRIBBLE
SCRIBBLE
SCRIBBLE

THE REST OF YOU— DRAW!! DRAW LIKE YOU'VE NEVER DRAWN BEFORE!

ART CLUB.

UUUGH...

i hate maaath.

DID YOU GET IT BACK?!

AFTER A LOT OF BEGGING AND PROMISES OF BONUS ASSIGNMENTS...

...YES.

MARIBELLA?

WHAT?

I THINK MY COMIC'S DONE.

....!

I-IT...

IT **IS** DONE.

I-I...

YEAH!!!

THAT'S TWO COMICS DONE!

WE'RE GONNA DO THIS!! JUST SIX COMICS TO FINISH BY THE END OF TODAY!!

FELICITY, WHAT'S YOUR STATUS?!

ON MY LAST PANEL! IT'S KINDA ROUGH, BUT...

IT'S FINE, IT'S FINE, AS LONG AS IT'S DONE!

...NATHANIEL, STATUS?

ER, HALFWAY?

ARGH!!

DONE.

...TYRONE?

LIKE A BOSS! YEAH, TYRONE!

SAM?

...WHERE'S SAM?

...OH, UM...

SAM'S... ER...

HE WENT HOME EARLY? HE SAID HE'S SICK.

SICK, HUH?

RIIIIGHT. CUTE TRICK.

TOO BAD I KNOW WHERE HE **LIVES**.

WHAT ABOUT YOU TWO? ALMOST DONE?

UH...

...I THINK WE HAVE A PROBLEM.

....!

THESE ARE TOO LONG!! AND NOT FINISHED!

I TOOOOOLD YOOOOU...

...OKAY, OKAY. LET'S THINK SOLUTIONS.

NINA, YOURS FIRST—CAN YOU CUT ANYTHING?

I ALREADY DID! THIS WAS WAY LONGER BEFORE.

MYSTERY of cafeteria food tray #1

GLOOP GLOOP

what's that? no idea

wait did it just move

RUN! RUN! it's gonna

quick! in here!

RAWR

AND THE FOURTH PANEL IS A CLIFFHANGER, SO I CAN'T JUST END IT THERE!

PEPPI.

YOU LOOK LIKE YOU HAVE AN IDEA!

...O-OH, UM... I WAS JUST THINKING, UH...

...THE PAGE THAT THE PAPER'S GIVING US—WILL WE GET THAT SPACE IN EVERY ISSUE?

YEAH. (AS LONG AS WE DON'T SCREW UP THIS DEADLINE.) WHY?

WELL...WHAT IF WE DID END IT WITH THIS PANEL...?

...AND THEN PUT "TO BE CONTINUED IN THE NEXT ISSUE"?

...!

BRILLIANT!

OMG, THIS WOULD TOTALLY WORK!!

YES!!

I CAN DO THAT FOR MINE TOO! I JUST HAVE TO...

BEST CO-EDITOR EVER!

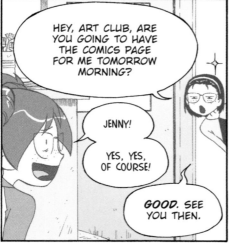

HEY, ART CLUB, ARE YOU GOING TO HAVE THE COMICS PAGE FOR ME TOMORROW MORNING?

JENNY!

YES, YES, OF COURSE!

GOOD. SEE YOU THEN.

OKAY, NO ONE LEAVES THIS ROOM WITHOUT FINISHING THEIR COMIC.

DRAW DRAW DRAW DRAW DRAW

LATER.

STILL PRETTY GOOD! AND WE CAN USE HIS IN THE NEXT ISSUE.

...ARGH. NATHANIEL COULDN'T FINISH, SO ONLY SEVEN COMICS...

YEAH, TRUE...

AND WE STILL HAVE ONE MORE COMIC TO PICK UP!

SAM'S HOUSE SHOULD BE AROUND...

HAHA HA HA
WHEE!
HA HA

SAM!

SAM O'REILLY!

....!

NOT SICK, I KNEW IT!!!

GIVE ME YOUR COMIC!!

...WHY DO YOU HAVE ONLY TWO PANELS DRAWN?

SAM'S ROOM.

DRAW DRAW

I-I WAS BUSY...

BUSY GOOFING OFF, ARGH!!

PEPPI, YOU HAVE SCIENCE HOMEWORK TO DO, RIGHT?

OKAY, SEE YOU TONIGHT!

YOU GO AHEAD. I'LL STAY AND MAKE SURE HE FINISHES.

7:30 P.M.

MY MOM SAID IT'S OKAY FOR ME TO SLEEP OVER!

YESSSS!!

BOUNCE BOUNCE

WE'RE GONNA FINISH THIS!!

WH-WHERE'S YOUR DAD?

HE'S AWAY ON A BUSINESS TRIP. IT'S JUST ME AND MY MOM HERE.

OH GOOD.

WAVE

HI, PENELOPE! MAKE YOURSELF AT HOME!

OKAY, WE NEED TO GIVE JENNY THE *COMPLETE* PAGE IN THE MORNING!

I'M READY. WHAT NEEDS TO BE DONE?

9:00 P.M.

TIC TOC TIC TOC

FINISHED PROOFING ALL THE DIALOGUE!

SWEET! HERE'S THE CORRECTIONS SET!

9:30 P.M.

TIC TOC TIC TOC

THESE ARE TAKING A WHILE...HOW'S THE TITLE GOING?

HALFWAY THROUGH INKING!

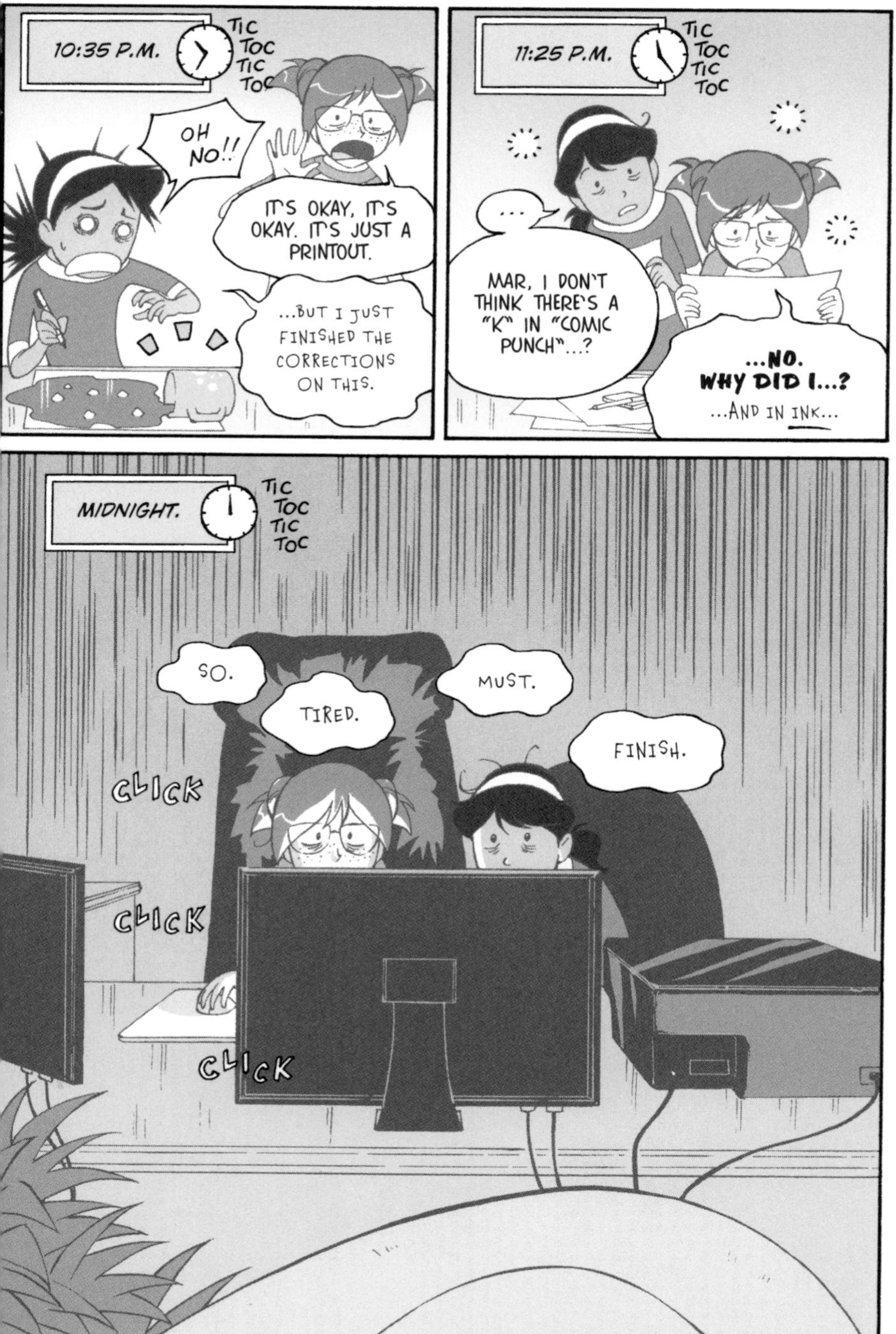
10:35 P.M.
TIC TOC TIC TOC
OH NO!!
IT'S OKAY, IT'S OKAY. IT'S JUST A PRINTOUT.
...BUT I JUST FINISHED THE CORRECTIONS ON THIS.
11:25 P.M.
TIC TOC TIC TOC
...
MAR, I DON'T THINK THERE'S A "K" IN "COMIC PUNCH"...?
...NO. WHY DID I...?
...AND IN INK...
MIDNIGHT.
TIC TOC TIC TOC
SO.
TIRED.
MUST.
FINISH.
CLICK
CLICK
CLICK

1:56 A.M.

...

...I CAN'T BELIEVE...
WE FINISHED...

...

YEAH...

...I CAN *NOT* TELL MY MOM HOW LATE WE STAYED UP. SHE'LL NEVER LET ME COME BACK.

...

PENELOPE?

...HNH?

THANK YOU.

FOR...

...NOT LEAVING ME ALONE...TO DEAL WITH THIS...

...WHEN THINGS GOT HARD.

OTHER PEOPLE WOULD HAVE.

YOU'RE A TRUE FRIEND.

...!

CHIRP CHIRP

...YOUR FRIDAY MORNING ANNOUNCEMENTS!

WHAT HAPPENED TO YOU?

A METRIC TON OF SPELLING MISTAKES IN PEOPLE'S COMICS, THAT'S WHAT.

WHO SPELLS "SCHOOL" AS "SHOOL"...?

gonna sleep so much this weekend...

DASH

OKAY, YOU GUYS, "COMIC PUNCH" IS HANDED IN!!

OH YEAH?!

AWESOMMME.

AND JENNY *LOVED IT!* SHE SAID IT'S THE BEST FEATURE THEY'VE EVER DONE!

WE'RE GONNA *CRUSH THE SCIENCE CLUB!*

YEEEAAH!!

WOO...

...yay?

...

BUT...

...JAIME'S IN THE SCIENCE CLUB...

143

LUNCH.

WAVE

hey, guys.

WAVE

....!

HEY, ART CLUB!

DID YOU SOLVE WORLD HUNGER WITH CARTOONS YET?

BLEEAH

HEY, JERK CLUB.

DID YOU RUIN ANOTHER SCHOOL EVENT FOR EVERYONE YET?!

man, why are they always sitting there?

◦MURMUR◦

ugh, i know, right?

just ignore them.

...

...IT'S LIKE WE'RE PART OF TWO RIVAL GANGS OR SOMETHING, GEEZ...

I DON'T FEEL LIKE IT'S OKAY TO EVEN SAY HI TO HIM...

WHY IS THIS SO COMPLICATED...?

SIGH

FLUTTER

WAH!

...A LETTER?
...FROM JAIME!

Hi Penelope,

My Mom was wondering it you and your family are free this Saturday. Would you want to come over for barbecue? She made an invitation and everything (because she is a dork). It's attached.

Jaime ":)"

P.S. We hid that geocache. If you come you can try to find it. ":)"

PSST

.....!

HEE HEE

OK!

HEY, PEPPI!

SHOVE

H-HEY, GUYS!

ARE YOU TRYING TO FIT YOURSELF IN YOUR LOCKER?

SATURDAY.

...I'M SO GLAD YOU COULD COME!

ARE YOU KIDDING? JAMES CAN'T SAY NO TO A BARBECUE.

C'MON, IT'S THIS WAY!

WHERE ARE YOU TWO GOING?

SHE WANTS TO FIND OUR GEOCACHE! I'M BORROWING MOM'S PHONE, OKAY?

ALL RIGHT. DON'T GO FAR.

??

♪

?

???

?!

...THAT'S SO COOL!

YEAH...I'M GONNA MISS THIS REMOTE. IT'S MY BEST ONE.

OH, ARE YOU GETTING RID OF IT?

KINDA? THAT'S THE REMOTE MY CLUB'S GONNA USE FOR THE...

...OOPS.

I'M NOT SUPPOSED TO TELL ANYONE.

... s-sorry.

..it's okay.

PSST

WE NEED TO FIND OUT WHAT THEY'RE MAKING!

nope

IT'S TOO BAD YOU HAVE TO GIVE YOURS AWAY.

YEAH...BUT MISS TOBINS IS REAL SERIOUS ABOUT WHAT THE PRINCIPAL SAID.

"CONTRIBUTING TO THE SCHOOL COMMUNITY" AND STUFF.

WE'RE ALL SUPPOSED TO HELP HOWEVER WE CAN...

...SO I'M GIVING THIS! THEY'RE KINDA PRICEY TO GET, AND WE NEED ONE FOR THE...

...UH.

...THING.

...

Awkward *adj.*
3. ...***THIS.***

...UH... YOU GUYS... ARE...DOING SOMETHING TOO, RIGHT? COMIC STRIPS?

OH! WE FINISHED! AT THE LAST MINUTE, HA-HA...

...BUT THE PAPER EDITOR LOVED IT!

OH YEAH?!

BET IT LOOKS AMAZING! I WANNA READ IT!

THANKS.

WE WORKED REAL HARD ON THAT.

...

...DO YOU CARE WHO GETS THE CLUB FAIR TABLE?

NO.

EVERYONE ELSE DOES, THOUGH. THIS COMPETITION IS SO *STUPID.*

YEAH.

JAIME! PEPPI! FOOD'S READY!

...AAAAND IT'S MONDAY AGAIN!

DLE SCHOOL

RI NG

STAGGER

GUYS.

....?

MARIBELLA, YOU OKAY?

THE SCIENCE CLUB...

...THEY FINALLY ANNOUNCED...

...THEIR PROJECT...

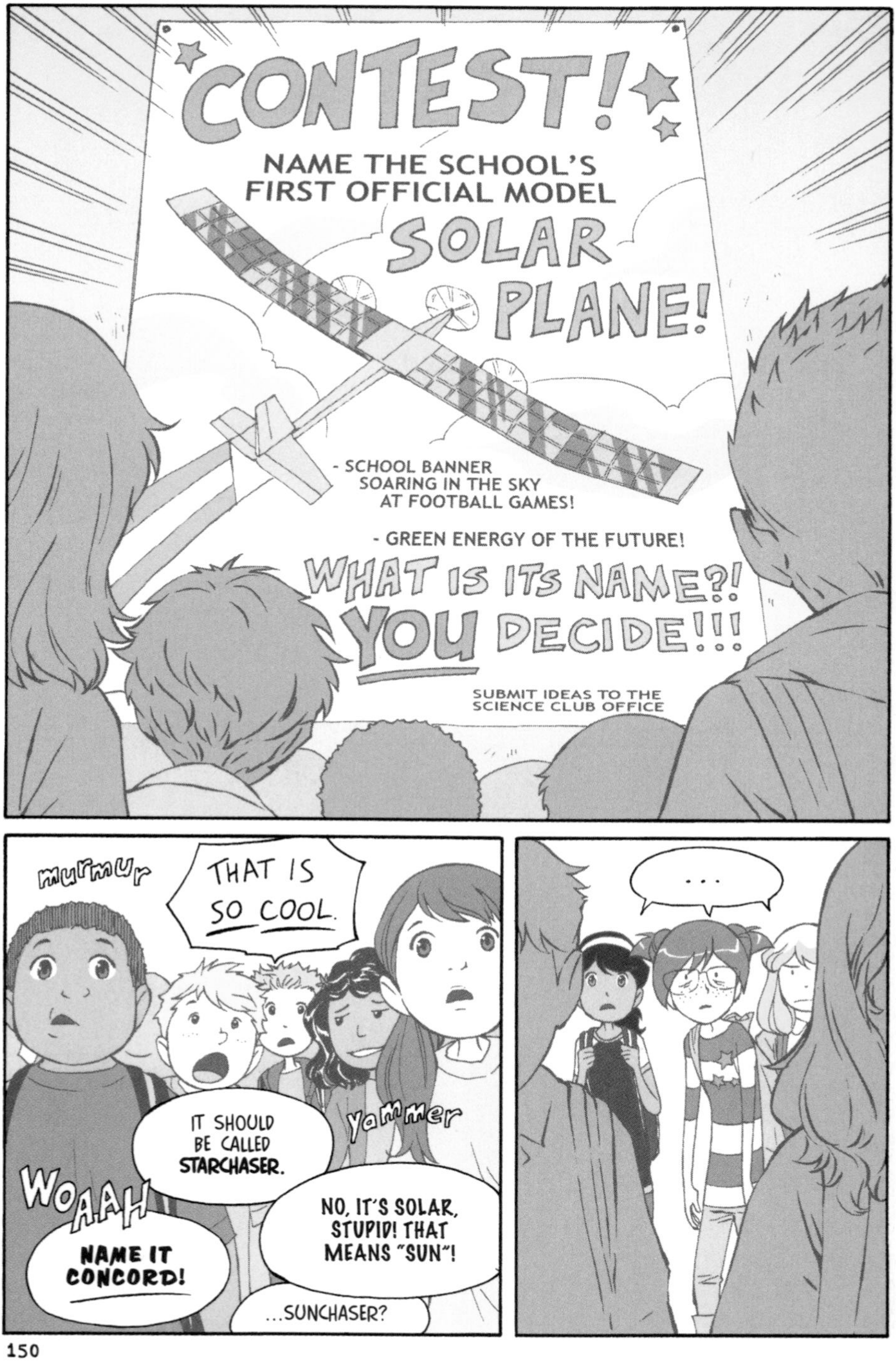
CONTEST!
NAME THE SCHOOL'S FIRST OFFICIAL MODEL
SOLAR PLANE!
- SCHOOL BANNER SOARING IN THE SKY AT FOOTBALL GAMES!
- GREEN ENERGY OF THE FUTURE!
WHAT IS ITS NAME?!
YOU DECIDE!!!
SUBMIT IDEAS TO THE SCIENCE CLUB OFFICE
murmur
THAT IS SO COOL.
yammer
IT SHOULD BE CALLED STARCHASER.
WOAAAH
NO, IT'S SOLAR, STUPID! THAT MEANS "SUN"!
NAME IT CONCORD!
...SUNCHASER?
...

YAMMED HA HA HA WINDSTRIDER HA

DID YOU SEE THE POSTERS?!

YEAH. SO AWESOME!

ARE YOU GONNA SUBMIT A NAME?

... THE WHOLE SCHOOL'S BUZZING.

WHATEVER. IT'S NOT *THAT* COOL.

...RIGHT?

IT IS SO COOL!

I'M GONNA SUBMIT THE NAME "SKYDOG"!!

WHAT??!

....

YOU'RE GONNA SUPPORT THEM?!!

WHOSE SIDE ARE YOU ON?!

....

I...

UH...

BUT IT'S A SOLAR PLANE !!!

HEY GUYS, HEY GUYS, I HAVE NEWS!!!

I WANT ONE...

JENNY AND AKILAH WERE SO IMPRESSED WITH "COMIC PUNCH" THAT THEY WANT MORE COMICS...

...FOR THE SCHOOL PAPER WEBSITE!

DO YOU GET IT?! EVEN MORE EXPOSURE! SO MORE PEOPLE VOTE FOR US!!

NOW, WHO'S GONNA DO ONE?!

COMICS AGAIN?!

MY HAND'S STILL HURTING FROM ALL THE DRAWING...

COMICS WERE TOO HAAAARD...

nOooo

MY BRAIN'S STILL HURTING.

...CAN WE JUST DRAW THEM SOME ELVES...?

n-no...

it has to be...

comics...

ART CLUB.

HWOOoo...

...IT'S SO LATE. IS NO ONE ELSE REALLY COMING?

LOOKS LIKE IT...

CLATTER

HA HA

WHOOPS

MISS T, JACK'S TRYING TO BREAK THE PLANE REMOTE!

I'M NOT! I DROPPED IT BY ACCIDENT!

WELL, BE CAREFUL!

PEEK

HEH HEH

...OH HEY, ART CLUB!

LOW TURNOUT TODAY?

DID EVERYONE ADMIT DEFEAT AND *QUIT*?

LATER.

STUPID SCIENCE CLUB.

CONTES

NAME THE SCHO FIRST OFFICIAL MO

SOLA PL

-SCHOOL BANNER SOARING IN THE SKY AT FOOTBALL GAMES!

- GREEN ENERGY OF TH

WHAT IS ITS

YOU DEC

SUBMIT IDEAS SCIENCE CLUB

CONTEST! ☆
NAME THE SCHOOL'S
FIRST OFFICIAL MODEL
SOLAR
PLANE!

—SCHOOL BANNER
SOARING IN THE SKY
AT FOOTBALL GAMES!
—GREEN ENERGY OF

...

...WE'RE
GONNA
LOSE...

...!

AWW, COME ON!
OUR COMICS ARE
PRETTY COOL...!
AND...AND WE'LL BE
DOING THE ONLINE
STUFF...!

...

...No, everyone's
gonna vote for this.

...How am I gonna
tell my dad...?

...

TUESDAY
MORNING.

BERRYBROOK MIDDLE SCHOOL

...ARE WE
REALLY GOING
TO LOSE?

IMPORTANT!! ART CLUB MEMBERS! THE PRINCIPAL TOLD ME THAT THE SCHOOL VOTE ON OUR PROJECTS WILL BE TOMORROW AFTER THE PLANE LAUNCH!

PLEASE BE THERE!

IT'S OUT!!!

THE PAPER WITH OUR COMICS!!!

FINALLY!!

OH WOW.

THIS LOOKS AMAZING! DID WE REALLY DO THAT?!

I NEED, LIKE, FIVE COPIES, HA-HA!

ME TOOOO

LOVE THISSS!

THAT'S GOOD, BUT...THE REAL TEST...

...IS WHAT THE SCHOOL THINKS.

HEE HEE

SO FUNNY.

WILL THERE BE MORE?

...

MAN, THIS "COMIC PUNCH" IS SO *STUPID*! THE "PICTURE DAY" ONE'S THE WORST. IS THAT SUPPOSED TO BE FUNNY?

THEY SHOULD NAME IT "COMIC FAIL," HA-HA!

...

PENELOPE!!

THESE WERE SO AWESOME!

YOUR GEOCACHING COMIC'S THE BEST ONE!

TH-THANKS!

WHEN ARE YOU GUYS DOING MORE?! THERE WERE TWO CLIFFHANGERS!

HUH!

MAYBE WE DO HAVE A CHANCE?

I DON'T KNOW WHAT TO THINK!!

SOME PEOPLE LOVED IT. SOME PEOPLE DIDN'T CARE...

I SAW SOMEONE THROW IT IN THE TRASH.

WHAT!

SO DID I.

NO.

really?

HA HA HA

CAN I HOLD IT?

HEY, I WANNA SEE, MOVE!

HEY, ONLY SCIENCE CLUB MEMBERS HAVE CLEARANCE TO TOUCH THE PLANE.

BUT EVERYONE CAN SEE IT FLY TOMORROW.

clearance? are you guys fbi or something, haha!

no, but my dad is.

WHAAAA!

OH, GREAT. THE SCIENCE CLUB HAS A FAN CLUB?

THEY'LL BE INSUFFERABLE NOW...

TUESDAY EVENING.

...I CAN'T FOCUS.

...ARE WE GONNA WIN?

OR IS THE SCIENCE CLUB?!

I DON'T WANT US TO LOSE, BUT...

SLUMP

PEPPI, YOUR FRIEND IS HERE TO SEE YOU!

...

FRIEND?

...JAIME? ☺

...!

MARIBELLA! WHAT...?

PEPPI, PLEASE HELP ME.

....!

HELP YOU WITH WHAT?

I-I... I took it.

I...

I saw it just lying on the table and I...

. . . !

shake

...THE PLANE REMOTE.

PLEASE, CAN YOU HELP ME HIDE IT?

WHY... WHY DID YOU TAKE...?

I-I JUST...

...I SAW IT THERE...

...AND I THOUGHT...

PLEASE HELP ME!!

MY DAD'S COMING BACK TONIGHT, AND HE CAN'T FIND OUT ABOUT THIS!!

don't disappoint me.

...

PLEASE, PENELOPE!! JUST UNTIL TOMORROW! I'LL FIGURE SOMETHING OUT TOMORROW...

...BUT I HAVE TO GET BACK HOME NOW BEFORE HE DOES!!

Please...I don't have anyone else to ask.

You're the only friend I have...

...!

...

...

...O-OKAY...

THANK YOU!!

I'LL TAKE IT BACK FIRST THING TOMORROW!

...

WHAT.

JUST.

HAPPENED?

CHAPTER 5

NEXT MORNING.

...OKAY, WHO'S EXCITED FOR THE SOLAR PLANE LAUNCH TODAY?!

...

...

DID YOU SEE THE SCIENCE CLUB? THEY'RE ACTING SO FREAKED OUT.

...

YEAH! THEY KEEP LOOKING EVERYWHERE FOR SOMETHING.

...

I KNOW WHAT THEY'RE LOOKING FOR...

...BUT THEY WON'T FIND IT.

BU-BUMP BU-BUMP

...BECAUSE IT'S IN. MY. BAG.

...ARGH! WHERE'S MARIBELLA?! SHE SHOULD'VE TAKEN IT BACK BY NOW!!

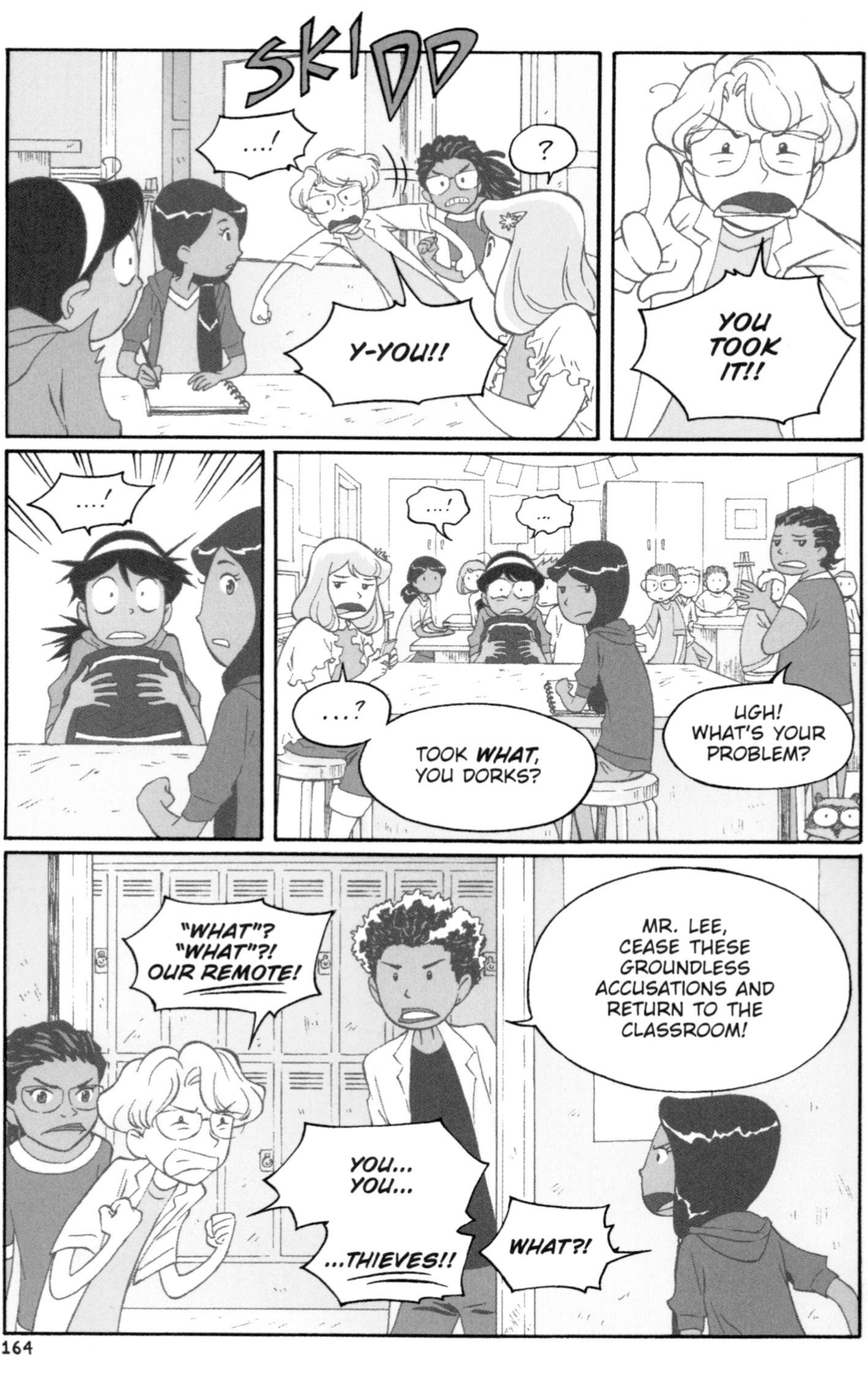
SKIDD
....!
?
Y-YOU!!
YOU TOOK IT!!
....!
....!
...
....?
TOOK WHAT, YOU DORKS?
UGH! WHAT'S YOUR PROBLEM?
"WHAT"? "WHAT"?! OUR REMOTE!
MR. LEE, CEASE THESE GROUNDLESS ACCUSATIONS AND RETURN TO THE CLASSROOM!
YOU... YOU...
...THIEVES!!
WHAT?!

...DOMINIC, THE REMOTE FOR THE SOLAR PLANE HAS BEEN MISPLACED. HAVE YOU—

....!

WHAT ARE YOU ACCUSING US OF?!

NO ONE IS ACCUSING ANYONE!!!

LOOK, I'M CERTAIN IT'S JUST AN ACCIDENT! PERHAPS THE CUSTODIANS PLACED IT IN THE WRONG CLASSROOM.

...

ALL I'M ASKING IS IF ANYONE HAS SEEN THE REMOTE, PLEASE LET ME KNOW, OKAY?

...

...

SCIENCE CLASS.

MARIBELLA NEVER SHOWED UP FOR HOMEROOM...

WHY AM I STUCK WITH THIS REMOTE?!!!

...I NEED TO DO SOMETHING.

...

MAYBE I SHOULD JUST GIVE IT TO MISS TOBINS LIKE SHE SAID?

...

...

...BUT WHAT IF SHE THINKS I TOOK IT...?

LUNCH.

I FEEL LIKE THE REMOTE'S GONNA BURN A HOLE IN MY BAG AND JUST **FALL OUT.**

HA-HA, THEY STILL HAVEN'T FOUND IT.

AND THE LAUNCH IS CANCELED UNTIL THEY DO!

CANCELED...?!

HEE HEE

...

HOW STUPID ARE THEY TO JUST LOSE A REMOTE LIKE THAT.

WE DIDN'T LOSE IT!! SOMEONE STOLE IT!

AND I'M SURE WE KNOW WHO!!

WHAT ARE YOU SAYING?!

YOU TOOK OUR REMOTE! THIEVES!!

. . . !

HOW DARE YOU! WE WOULD NEVER—

YOU DID, YOU DID! YOU TOOK IT! YOU KNEW WE WERE GONNA WIN!

WE DIDN'T TAKE YOUR STUPID REMOTE!!!

. . .

ART CLUB.

MR. R? HAVE YOU SEEN MARIBELLA TODAY?!

NO, I THINK SHE'S OUT SICK.

. . .

...SICK, HUH? RIIIIIIGHT.

GUYS, DID YOU SEE THE SCHOOL PAPER WEBSITE?

HUH?

NO.

WHY?

ART CLUB SABOTAGED THE LAUNCH OF THE SCHOOL SOLAR PLANE. THEY'RE LIARS AND CHEATS!!!

GASP!!

....!

WHA——?! WHO...?

IT WASN'T US! SOMEONE HACKED OUR WEBSITE AND POSTED THAT!

SOMEONE?! HA! WE KNOW EXACTLY WHO!

GRAB

WELL, WE'LL SHOW THEM!

C'MON, GUYS! GRAB SOME PAINT AND BRUSHES!

WE'LL HACK THEIR POSTERS TO SAY SOMETHING ELSE TOO!

NO NO NO

THIS HAS TO STOP!!

MARIBELLA STARTED THIS...

...AND **SHE'S** GOING TO END IT. HER AND HER GREAT IDEAS.

SKIDDD

MARIBELLA!

KNOCK

DING-DONG DING-DONG

KNOCK

MRS. SAMSON?!

HELLOOO!

WHY ISN'T ANYONE ANSWERING?!

MARIBELLA!

COME ON, OPEN UP!!

HELLO?

....?

ARE YOU LOOKING FOR THE SAMSON FAMILY?

U-UH, YEAH, I...

I'M SO SORRY, DEAR, BUT THEY'RE GONE.

WHA...?

THERE WAS A BIG FIGHT HERE YESTERDAY. A LOT OF YELLING AND SCREAMING...

I SAW THE WIFE AND THE LITTLE GIRL GET IN THE CAR AND LEAVE.

BOTH HAD BAGS PACKED, SO IT LOOKED LIKE THEY MIGHT BE GONE AWHILE.

. . .

WHAAAAT?

SQUEAK SQUEAK

SQUEAK

. . .

STOP

...

I'M ON MY OWN WITH THIS.

EVENING.

PEPPI, DINNER IS READY!

PEPPIIIII!

...

I CAN'T KEEP IT HERE.

SHOULD I JUST THROW IT OUT?

NO ONE WOULD EVER KNOW.

...THEN THEY WOULDN'T BE ABLE TO FLY THEIR PLANE.

THE ART CLUB WOULD WIN FOR SURE, THEN.

...

...THAT'S... GOOD... RIGHT...?

EXCEPT IT WOULDN'T REALLY BE...

...FAIR.

...AND WE'D BE LIARS AND CHEATERS, JUST LIKE THEY SAID.

...WE ARE NOT LIARS AND CHEATERS.

I'M GONNA FIX THIS.

JAIME'S HOUSE.

...

...O-OKAY... ALL I HAVE TO DO IS...

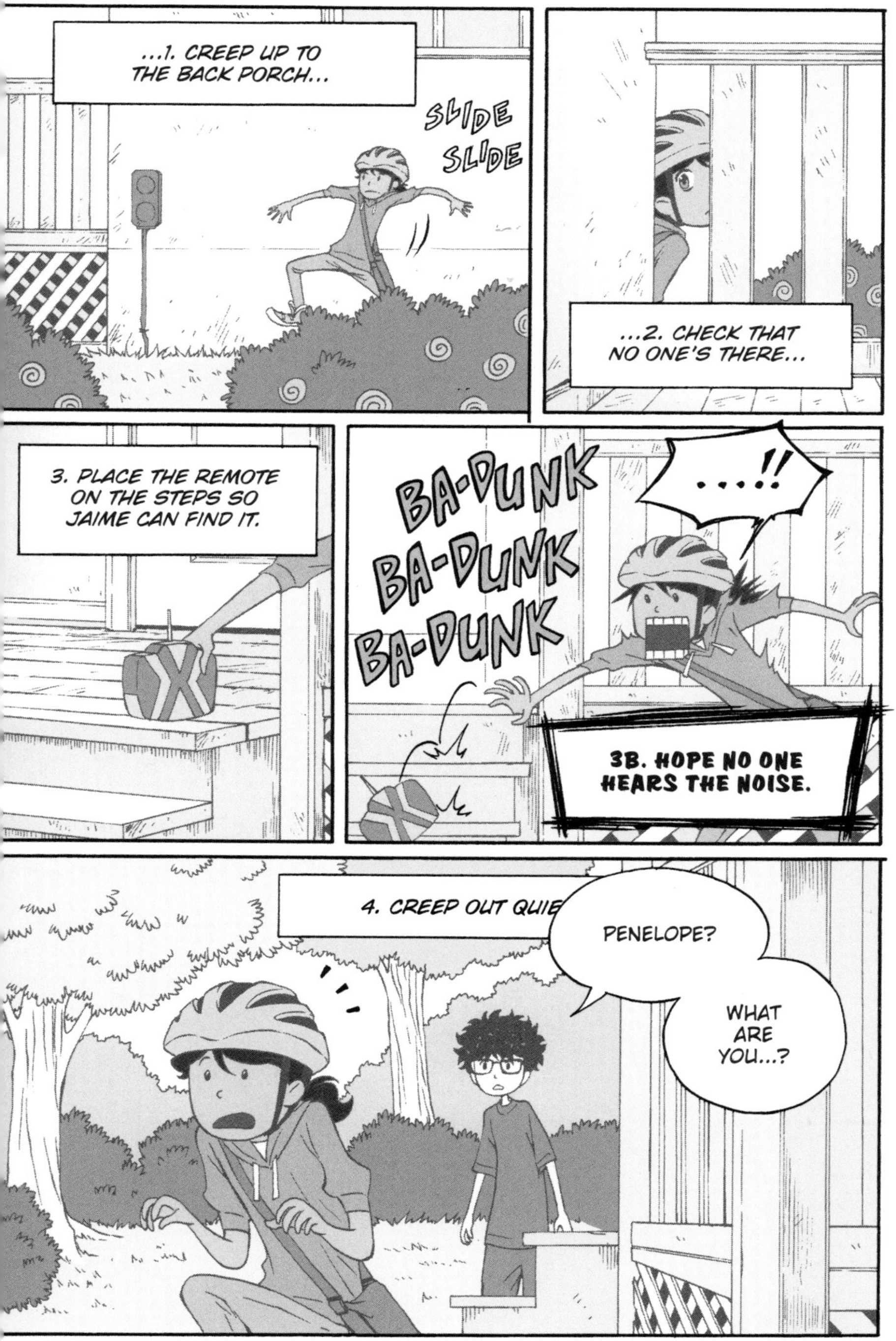
...1. CREEP UP TO THE BACK PORCH...
SLIDE SLIDE
...2. CHECK THAT NO ONE'S THERE...
3. PLACE THE REMOTE ON THE STEPS SO JAIME CAN FIND IT.
BA-DUNK BA-DUNK BA-DUNK
...!!
3B. HOPE NO ONE HEARS THE NOISE.
4. CREEP OUT QUIE
PENELOPE?
WHAT ARE YOU...?

....!

THAT'S OUR REMOTE!

YOU TOOK IT?!!

WH-WHA—!

NO!

IT WASN'T ME!

WE...WE WORKED SO HARD ON THAT PLANE!!

WHY WOULD YOU GUYS STEAL OUR REMOTE?!!

IT WASN'T US!

...WELL...

...IT WAS ONE OF US...

WHO?!

...

ARGH

I...

I CAN'T TELL YOU!!

SHE'S A FRIEND!

YOU'RE FRIENDS WITH A THIEF?!!

...!

N-NO!

IT'S NOT LIKE THAT!

THEN WHAT'S IT LIKE?!

SHE'S...

SHE'S NOT A BAD PERSON!

SHE JUST...

SHE PANICKED!

AND... MADE A MISTAKE.

YOU KNOW...

LIKE...

LIKE I DID.

...!

WHEN I PUSHED YOU.

...

...

I BET SHE'D BRING IT BACK HERSELF IF SHE COULD.

I'M...

I'M REALLY SORRY SHE TOOK IT FROM YOU GUYS.

...

OKAY.

THANKS FOR GIVING THIS BACK.

BYE.

...

...THIS...

...DIDN'T GO WELL AT ALL.

THE MISSING REMOTE'S BEEN FOUND!

IN THE LIBRARY, OF ALL PLACES! HOW'D IT END UP THERE?

BUT, HEY, WHATEVER. BECAUSE GUESS WHAT THIS MEANS...

...THE SOLAR PLANE LAUNCH IS BACK ON!!!

SOAR

murmur

murmur

so cool

VMMMMM

OH, WOOOOW, IT'S AMAZING!

GO, SKYDOG!!

HIGHER! HIGHER!

...

THEY DID WORK HARD ON THAT...

IT LOOKS GREAT.

They picked my name!!

Go, Skydog!!

CAFETERIA.

THAT PLANE WAS INCREDIBLE.

YEAH.

I GUESS WE'RE NOT GETTING THE CLUB FAIR TABLE THIS YEAR, THEN.

AW, COME ON!

THEY DIDN'T EVEN DO THE VOTE YET! WE STILL HAVE A CHANCE!

NO WAY WE'LL WIN.

...

...I GUESS NOT.

BUT...

...ART CLUB'S STILL THE BEST PART OF MY DAY.

WELL, WHATEVER. WHO NEEDS THAT TABLE ANYWAY. WE'LL HAVE OUR OWN FUN.

HEY, LOOK WHAT I DREW!

IS IT A SUNSPOT?

HA HA

N-NO!

HA HA

OKAY, GUYS! STOP TEASING HIM!

A SPACE STATION?! JENSEN, THAT'S SO COOL!

STAGGER

OOOH!

IS THIS FOR A COMIC?

DUNNO. MAYBE?

MR. R!

WHAT WERE THE RESULTS OF THE VOTE?!

DO YOU KNOW YET?

...

There...was no vote...

...and there will not be one...

WHA...?!

The principal... will explain...

ART CLUB.

SCIENCE CLUB.

GREETINGS.

THANK YOU FOR WORKING SO HARD ON YOUR PROJECTS.

THEY ARE BOTH OUTSTANDING AND SOME OF THE BEST CONTRIBUTIONS THIS SCHOOL HAS EVER SEEN.

HOWEVER...

...DUE TO THE UNSPORTSMANLIKE CONDUCT DISPLAYED BY BOTH SIDES...

.....!!

...NEITHER OF YOU WILL HAVE A TABLE AT THE CLUB FAIR.

WHA——!

HUH?!

THE POINT OF THE FAIR IS TO CELEBRATE AND SUPPORT THE ACCOMPLISHMENTS OF YOUR FELLOW STUDENTS.

...

...

BUT BOTH YOUR CLUBS FAILED TO SHOW THAT SPIRIT. INSTEAD...

...YOU HAVE SHOWN DISDAIN AND EVEN OUTRIGHT HATRED TOWARD EACH OTHER.

IT IS A PROBLEM.

WHILE I CONSIDER HOW TO SOLVE THIS...

...I AM SUSPENDING ALL YOUR CLUB ACTIVITIES UNTIL FURTHER NOTICE.

COLLECT YOUR THINGS.

GO HOME.

GOOD DAY. →CLICK←

....!

GASP!!!

.....!!

WH-WHA...?

...MR. R?!!

IT'S TRUE... THE ART CLUB IS SUSPENDED...

THE SCIENCE CLUB TOO...

JUST LIKE THAT?!

BUT...!!

IT'S NO USE ARGUING.

EVERYONE, JUST...

...GO HOME.

...

ART ROOM

... murmur

whaaa...

CAN'T BELIEVE THIS IS HAPPENING...

IS THIS FOR REAL...?

... !

YOU!!

THIS IS ALL YOUR FAULT!!

WHAT?

YOU WERE THE ONES CAUSING PROBLEMS!!

YOU HACKED THE SCHOOL WEBSITE!!

YOU SABOTAGED OUR LAUNCH!!

WHAT THE...?!

NO, WE DIDN'T!!

YES, YOU DID!!

...

...

YOU PUT DETERGENT PACKS IN OUR SINKS!!

WELL, YOU DREW ON OUR DOOR!!

...

YOU'RE CONCEITED JERKS!!

YOU'RE THE JERKS, YOU STUPID—

STOPPIT!!!

JUST...

JUST STOP IT, ALL OF YOU!!

...

...A-ALL THIS FIGHTING...

LOOK WHERE IT GOT US...

NONE OF US HAVE A CLUB ANYMORE!!

DASH

...

...!

...THIS IS SO STUPID...!

I WANT THE ART CLUB BACK!!

WHY IS THIS HAPPENING??

WE WORKED SO HARD!!

...HUH?

WHOSE CAR IS...?

PEPPI!

YOUR FRIEND IS HERE TO VISIT!

. . .

. . . . !

MARIBELLA.

YOU GIRLS CATCH UP!

I'LL GO CHAT WITH MRS. SAMSON.

. . .

I...

I came back...

...for the remote?

. . .

UH.

ACTUALLY...

...I GAVE IT BACK.

....!

OH, GOOD.

SLUMP

I SNUCK IT BACK TO THEM...THEY DON'T KNOW IT WAS YOU.

MAR, WHAT HAPPENED?!

YOU WEREN'T IN SCHOOL OR AT CLUB...

I WENT TO YOUR HOUSE, BUT YOUR NEIGHBOR SAID YOU AND YOUR MOM LEFT?

M-my parents, they...

They had a huge fight...

I've never... heard them yell at each other like that before.

Now my mom and I are staying with my uncle...

...BUT WE'RE LEAVING TOMORROW TO GO LIVE WITH MY GRANDMA FOR A WHILE...

....!

AND SHE'S, LIKE, *TWO STATES* AWAY!

WHA...? WHEN ARE YOU COMING BACK?

... I... I don't know...

· · ·

MARIBELLA, SWEETHEART, IT'S TIME TO GO!

COULD... COULD I WRITE YOU? IS THAT OKAY?

OF COURSE, YEAH!

I DIDN'T GET TO TELL HER...

BYE.

...THAT THE ART CLUB GOT SUSPENDED.

IT'S FRIDAY MORNING! ARE YOU READY FOR THE WEEKEND?!

. . .

. . .

...EVERYONE'S ACTING WEIRD BECAUSE I YELLED AT THEM YESTERDAY.

WHATEVER.

I MEANT WHAT I SAID. THIS FIGHTING HAS TO STOP.

LUNCH.

. . .

GLOOM

WE ALL WANT THE ART CLUB BACK.

BUT HOW?

GLOOM

...I BET THEY WANT THEIR CLUB BACK TOO.

think think think

NNNGH.

FRIDAY'S OVER, YEAAAAH!

SEE YOU GUYS MONDAY!

DID TESSA AND NINA LEAVE WITHOUT ME...?

GUESS I'M GOING HOME BY MYSELF TODAY.

SIGH

EVERYTHING'S SUCH A MESS.

BUMP

WAH!

PENELOPE! HELLO.

GAH!! I'M SO SORRY! I WASN'T LOOKING!!

IT'S ALL RIGHT. ARE YOU HEADING HOME TOO?

Y-YEAH.

FEELS STRANGE NOT TO BE GOING TO OUR CLUBS RIGHT NOW, HUH?

...

I'VE BEEN MEANING TO SAY, YOU'VE BEEN DOING *EXCELLENT* WORK IN MY CLASS!

ARE YOU KEEPING UP WITH YOUR ART AS WELL?

Y-YES, MA'AM. STRAIGHT A's.

DOING WELL IN ART AND SCIENCE! YOU'RE A REAL RENAISSANCE GIRL, MISS TORRES!

A RENAISSANCE PERSON IS... SOMEONE WHO IS ACCOMPLISHED IN SEVERAL DIFFERENT FIELDS.

LIKE A MUSICIAN WHO IS ALSO AN ARCHITECT AND A PHILOSOPHER.

..."RENAISSANCE GIRL"?

WHAT'S THAT?

...OR, ANOTHER EXAMPLE—DID YOU KNOW THAT THERE ARE ARTISTS WHO ARE ALSO SCIENTISTS?

...SERIOUSLY?

YEP! LEONARDO DA VINCI WAS ONE.

HE'S A VERY FAMOUS PAINTER WHO LIVED HUNDREDS OF YEARS AGO IN ITALY.

HIS PAINTINGS ARE CONSIDERED MASTERPIECES AND ARE EXHIBITED IN THE WORLD'S BEST MUSEUMS...

189

HE BUILT FLYING MACHINE PROTOTYPES, STUDIED HUMAN ANATOMY AND PLANTS...

...BUT HE WAS ALSO A SCIENTIST, A MATHEMATICIAN, AND AN ENGINEER.

BASICALLY, AN ALL-AROUND SCIENCE GEEK.

...!

LIKE WITH MY MERMAID DRAWING!

WHEN I DREW HER SKELETON?

THAT'S EXACTLY RIGHT! THE INTERSECTION OF ART AND SCIENCE!

...BECAUSE THEY REALLY AREN'T THAT DIFFERENT, YOU KNOW.

I WISH OUR CLUBS COULD SEE THAT.

MAYBE THEN THEY WOULDN'T FIGHT SO MUCH.

SIGH

...!

...

WELL, ANYWAY.

KEEP UP THE GOOD WORK, MISS TORRES!

BYE.

...ARTISTS WHO ARE ALSO SCIENTISTS, HUH...?

WEEKEND.

PEPPI?

YOU'VE BEEN IN YOUR ROOM FOR HOURS! IS EVERYTHING OKAY?

YES, MOM!

DOING HOMEWORK!

...HOMEWORK OF DOOM!

BECAUSE I JUST MAAAAY HAVE AN IDEA.

IT'S A STUPID IDEA. AND KIND OF CRAZY.

...BUT IF MOVIES HAVE TAUGHT ME ANYTHING, IT'S THAT IF THE IDEA IS STUPID AND CRAZY ENOUGH...

...IT JUST. MIGHT. WORK.

I JUST HAVE TO... GET EVERYONE ELSE TO GO ALONG.

SOMEHOW.

OH, PEPPIIIII!

GUESS WHO'S HERE TO SEEEE YOU!

...

...

...

Is that... tone... necessary...?

SOON.

...

Awkward adj.
4. ...*THESE TWO FOREVER*.

S-SORRY MY MOM'S AN *EMBARRASSING* DORK. Ugh.

...S'OKAY. MINE'S THE SAME.

...

UM.

I CAME TO SAY...SORRY.

HUH? FOR WHAT?

YOU BROUGHT BACK THE REMOTE...AND I YELLED AT YOU.

OH.

SURE.

IT'S...IT'S OKAY.

THANKS FOR NOT TELLING ANYONE ABOUT THAT.

SLUMP

...NOT THAT IT HELPED ANYTHING. THEY STILL THINK YOU GUYS DID IT. AND EVERYONE'S FIGHTING.

I HATE IT.

...

YEAH.

...BUT I THINK I HAVE AN IDEA TO FIX THAT.

WANNA HELP ME?

JAIME WOULD BE THE **PERFECT** ALLY FOR THIS.

HE'S IN SCIENCE, I'M IN ART...

...BUT WE'RE **FRIENDS.**

IT'S WHAT THE PRINCIPAL SAID HE WANTED FOR OUR CLUBS.

HE'S JUST BEEN GOING ABOUT IT WRONG.

THAT'S **BRILLIANT.** I'M IN.

YAAAY!

NOW WE JUST NEED TO FIGURE OUT HOW TO GET THEM ALL IN ONE PLACE.

HEH-HEH, HOW MUCH PAPER DO YOU HAVE?

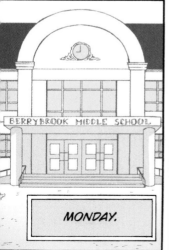

BERRYBROOK MIDDLE SCHOOL

MONDAY.

TESSA.

NINA.

PLOP

....!

193

DO YOU GUYS WANT THE ART CLUB BACK?

...Y-YEAH?

THEN YOU GOTTA HELP ME.

WE NEED TO GET THE ART CLUB AND THE SCIENCE CLUB TO MEET TODAY AFTER SCHOOL.

SO WE NEED TO PUT THESE IN ALL THEIR LOCKERS.

THE SCIENCE CLUB?! WHA—

YES, THE SCIENCE CLUB! WE NEED THEM FOR THIS, OKAY?

BUT...

JUST DO IT PLEASE!

I'LL EXPLAIN EVERYTHING LATER!

HMPF

GRUMBLE ...okay.

THIS IS NOT GOING TO BE EASY...

...I'M SO GLAD I'M NOT ON MY OWN WITH THIS.

AFTER SCHOOL.

grumble mutter hmpf

194

murmur

murmur

what are THEY doing here?

what's this about anyway?

...H-HELLO?

TURN

TURN

...

U-UH.

...OKAY, OKAY, I CAN DO THIS. JUST CONVINCE EVERYONE TO...

WAVE

...H-HELLO!

TH-THANK YOU ALL FOR COMING.

UM, I...

THE PAPER WE GOT SAID THERE'S A WAY TO GET OUR CLUB BACK. IS THAT TRUE?

...U-UH, YES? WELL, WHAT I MEAN IS—

THE PRINCIPAL HIMSELF SAID THE CLUBS ARE CANCELED. HOW ARE YOU GONNA—

WELL, MAYBE IF YOU GUYS LET HER **TALK**, WE'D FIND OUT?

...

GO AHEAD, PEPPI! TELL US YOUR IDEA!

U-UH...

BU-BUMP

BU-BUMP

OH GOD, EVERYONE'S LOOKING AT MEEEEEE.

I'VE JUST BEEN THINKING...

INHALE

...

TH-THE PRINCIPAL SAID THAT HE WANTS US TO STOP FIGHTING...A-AND CONTRIBUTE TO THE SCHOOL COMMUNITY.

S-SO I THOUGHT...

...HOW ABOUT...

...W-WE DO A JOINT PROJECT?

MAKE SOMETHING TOGETHER, BOTH CLUBS?

....!

WHAAAAAT...?!

US WORKING WITH **THEM**?

WHAT, DID YOU GUYS SUDDENLY LEARN TO **SCIENCE** OR SOMETHING?

OH, DID YOU LEARN TO **ART**?

L-LOOK, I KNOW HOW THIS SOUNDS, BUT...THINK ABOUT IT!

IF WE PROVE WE CAN WORK TOGETHER...

...THE PRINCIPAL WILL *HAVE* TO GIVE BACK OUR CLUBS!

....!

ARGH. THEY'RE ALL SO STUBBORN!

LOOK, WE'RE SCIENTISTS.

YOU GUYS ARE ARTSY-FARTSY PEOPLE.

IT JUST DOESN'T WORK.

NOD NOD

W-WELL, YEAH, BUT... I MEAN...

S-SCIENCE AND ART AREN'T THAT DIFFERENT, OKAY?

....!

DID YOU KNOW THAT DURING, LIKE... RENAISSANCE?

THERE WERE FAMOUS ARTISTS WHO WERE ALSO SCIENTISTS?

OH, YOU MEAN THAT DA VINCI GUY, RIGHT?

...

YES, YES! HIM!

A-AND OTHERS!

...SO?

REMEMBER GEOCACHING?

YES, THAT'S RIGHT! WE WORKED TOGETHER THEN!

AND WE GOT *FIRST PLACE!*

OH YEAH!

...!

HEH HEH

WE DID ROCK THAT! THAT WAS A GOOD ONE!

REMEMBER THOSE TWO GUYS AND THE TERRARIU—

ANYWAY.

...THE POINT IS...!

IF WE CAN PROVE THAT WE CAN WORK TOGETHER...

...WE CAN GET OUR CLUBS BACK!

murmur huh!

that's true.

murmur maybe that WOULD work.

BUT...

...WHAT COULD WE DO? I MEAN, ART AND SCIENCE, UH...

...WHAT WOULD THE PROJECT BE?

...OKAY, GOOD, GOOD. I GOT THEM AT LEAST CONSIDERING IT...!

OH! WE HAVE THIS IDEA FOR ONE!

JAIME?

UN RO LL

WH-WHAT DO YOU GUYS THINK ABOUT...

UN RO LL

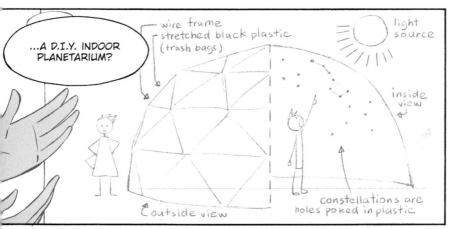

...A D.I.Y. INDOOR PLANETARIUM?

wire frame
stretched black plastic (trash bags)

light source

inside view

outside view

constellations are holes poked in plastic.

WHAAA...

can we even do that?

hey, stop blocking.

...

...THEY...THEY SEEM TO LIKE IT?

IS THIS...ACTUALLY GONNA WORK?

PLEASE, PLEAAASE WORK...

TURN

...

...

THIS. IS. AMAZING.

WHERE DO WE SIGN UP?

YESSSSS!

WAIT, BUT HOW IS THIS AN ART PROJECT?

... nooooooo.

I AM SO GLAD YOU ASKED.

YOU DON'T LOOK GLAD...

OKAY, SEE HOW THIS THING IS KINDA SAD AND DRAB-LOOKING?

WHAT. NO. IT'S AMAZING.

I MEAN, C'MON, IT'S TRASH BAGS AND WIRE WITH HOLES.

HA-HA, YEAH!

HEY!

WE COULD DESIGN IT INTO AN ACTUAL EXHIBIT!

LIKE THOSE COOL ONES AT THE DISCOVERY CENTER WITH PAINTED BACKGROUNDS?

COULD WE DO CONCEPTUAL SCULPTURES? OF, LIKE, STAR SYSTEMS OR WHATEVER?

YES! YES! WHATEVER YOU WANT!

I ALMOST HAVE THEM!!

OHHH! WE COULD DO GIANT BACKDROPS OF THE MILKY WAY!

HUH!

YEAH! OR EVEN...

IIIII GET IT! SO WE'LL MAKE THEIR BORING STUFF LOOK PRETTY?

YES!

BORING?!!

...NO?

...

YOU'RE _BORING!!_

WE DON'T EVEN _NEED_ YOU ARTS AND CRAFTS, OKAY?!

ARGH! NO, NO, NO, I ALMOST HAD THEM!!!

C'MON, GUYS! COOPERATION, NOT FIGHTING!

THINK ABOUT GETTING YOUR CLUBS BACK!

STOP FIGHTING!

SEVERAL CENTURIES LATER.

-HWOOOoo..

...

...I CAN'T BELIEVE...

...YOU GOT THEM ALL TO SIGN UP.

IT...

IT WORKED.

...I CAN'T FEEL MY BONES.

NEXT MORNING.

WE SHOWED THE PROJECT TO MISS TOBINS AND MR. R...

...AND MISS TOBINS **LOVED** IT. (MR. R MOSTLY LOOKED CONFUSED BUT HAPPY.)

THEY TOOK IT TO THE PRINCIPAL...

TIC TOC TIC TOC TIC TOC TIC

...AND AFTER WHAT FELT LIKE FOREVER...

...HE SAID **YES**, BUILD THIS, AND HE'LL UNCANCEL OUR CLUBS!

YEEEEAAAH!!

HE APPARENTLY ALSO CRIED HAPPY LITTLE TEARS...

...SINCE WE WEREN'T GOING TO FIGHT ANYMORE.

WHICH WASN'T EASY AT FIRST.

SQUIRT

OF COURSE, THERE WAS STILL FIGHTING.

BUT IT GOT BETTER.

BIT BY BIT.

AND WE WORKED OUR **BUTTS** OFF ON THIS THING.

WE EVEN HAD TO TAKE PARTS HOME SO WE COULD FINISH ON TIME.

BUT THE RESULT...

...WAS SO. WORTH. IT.

PLANETARIUM
★PRIZES!
GUESS 3 OR 4
CONSTELLATIONS

WORM H

WOW.

THE PRINCIPAL DID GIVE US TABLES AT THE FAIR, BUT UNDER ONE CONDITION...

...THAT WE SIT TOGETHER.

WHICH WORKED OUT WELL.

MOSTLY.

...ONCE WE GOT DEREK AND NATHANIEL TO STOP COMPETING ABOUT HOW HIGH THE CLUB SIGNS WERE.

BUT AT LEAST JAIME AND I CAN BE PROPER FRIENDS NOW.

...THE CONSTELLATIONS ARE ALL LISTED, AND THERE'S A BLANK PAGE IN THE BACK TO MAKE YOUR OWN.

YAAAAY!

CAFETERIA.

CHATTER HA HA! HEY CHATTER CHATTER

DID YOU GO TO THE CLUB FAIR?

YEAH!! DID YOU SEE THE PLANETARIUM?!

...NOW WE HAVE TO THINK OF SOMETHING EVEN COOLER FOR NEXT YEAR.

I DUNNO, THAT'S HARD TO TOP.

...MAYBE A SPACESHIP!

WHAAAT?!

IF WE SHOOK UP ENOUGH SODA CANS...

...ATTACHED THEM TO SOMETHING...

...OPENED THEM ALL AT THE SAME TIME...

I'M SERIOUS! IT WOULD BREAK THROUGH THE ATMOSPHERE!

AND LAND ON THE MOON!

HA-HA-HA!

WAIT, WAIT...

...LIKE THIS?

moon

whee!

HA-HA, YESSS, PERFECT!

! HEY, WHAT'S *THIS*?

NERDER GIRLFRIEND IS DRAWING SPACESHIPS NOW?

....!

AWWWW, ARE YOU PLANNING YOUR HONEYMOON...

...ON THE *MOOON*?

HA-HA! "HONEYMOON ON THE MOON," GOOD ONE!

S-STOP BULLYING US!

HA HA HA

GIVE THAT BACK!

SAY PLEASE, NERDER GIRLFRIEND!

HA HA HA

HEY, JERKBRAINS.

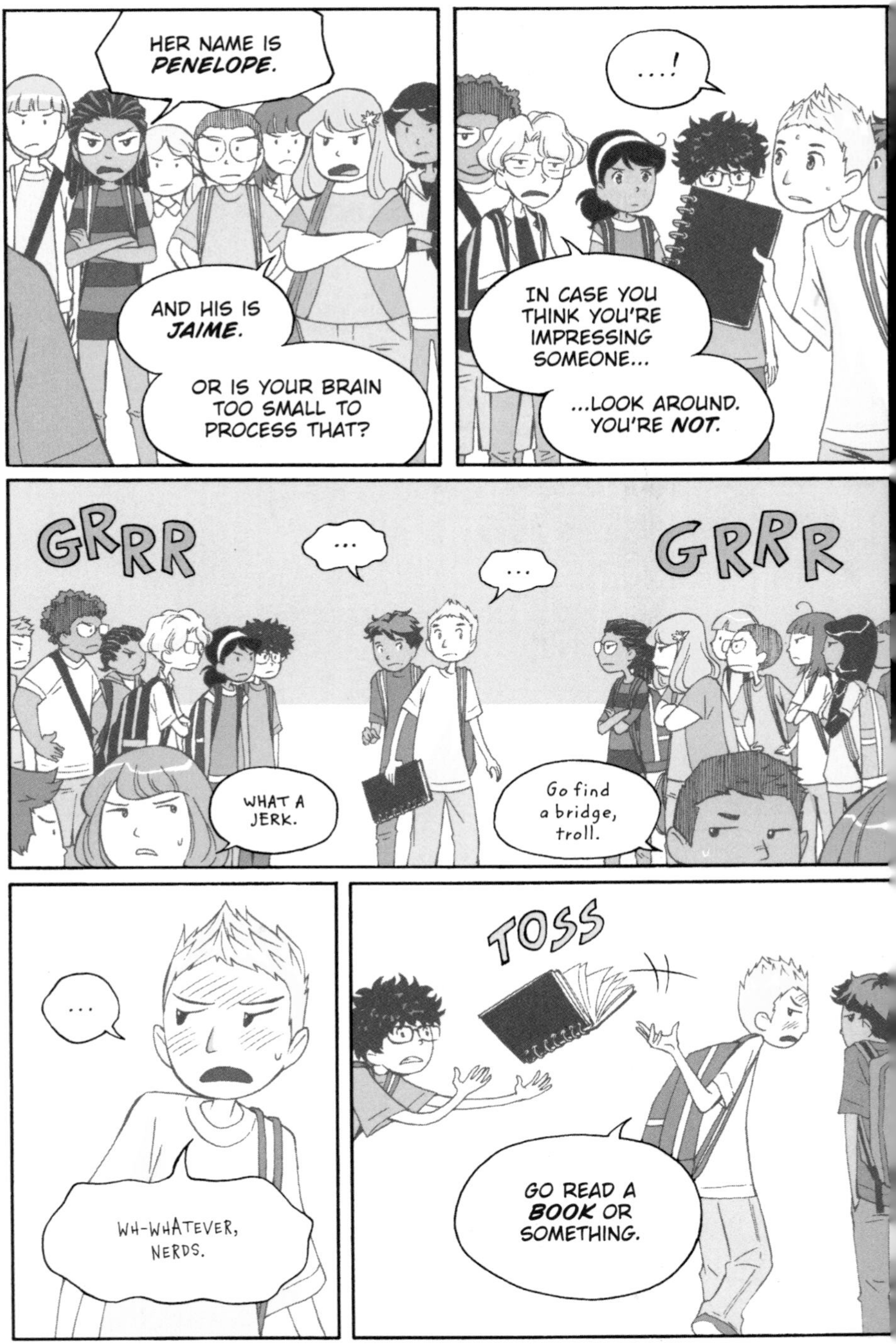
HER NAME IS PENELOPE.
AND HIS IS JAIME.
OR IS YOUR BRAIN TOO SMALL TO PROCESS THAT?
. . . !
IN CASE YOU THINK YOU'RE IMPRESSING SOMEONE...
...LOOK AROUND. YOU'RE NOT.
GRRR
...
...
GRRR
WHAT A JERK.
Go find a bridge, troll.
...
WH-WHATEVER, NERDS.
TOSS
GO READ A BOOK OR SOMETHING.

"GO READ A BOOK™"?! IS THAT SUPPOSED TO BE AN INSULT?

I DUNNO. I DON'T SPEAK CAVEMAN.

ARE YOU OKAY?

...

YEAH.

THANKS.

I HAVE GREAT FRIENDS.

SO, WHAT ARE WE DOING NEXT?

WE NEED A PROJECT!

OHH, OHHH, I HAVE AN IDEA.

CHATTER

HEY, THAT'S *MY* SEAT!

WE MAY HAVE OUR PROBLEMS, BUT...

HA HA

CHATTER

CH

...IT ALL COMES DOWN TO...

...CARDINAL RULE #3 FOR SURVIVING SCHOOL:

BUILD.

BUILD THINGS.

BUILD FRIENDSHIPS.

BUILD YOURSELF.

BIT BY LITTLE BIT.

IT MAY FEEL LIKE YOU'RE NOT ADDING THAT MUCH...

...BUT IN THE END, IT WILL ADD UP TO A LOT.

THE END

Meet the author

Hellooooo! I hope you enjoyed reading this book as much as I did making it!! Comics are so great. I still can't believe sometimes that drawing comics all day is my job...

Me, 11 years old (in Crimea)
(with bonus random monkey. I do NOT remember where it came from...)

And I started out just like Peppi—scribbling drawings in my science notebooks and submitting my art to the school newspaper! I went through a period where I'd draw my family and the family pets as droplets with arms and legs and reeeeally long stick noses:

me →
our dog
the cat

baby sis   mom   dad

... I still draw like this sometimes, but I hope that I've leveled up somewhat in my artistic skills since then? You read the book, so you be the judge!!

In the meantime, I have some wonderful people to thank... I get fanmail sometimes, which really perks me up, but another great source of love and support in my life are people who are kind of like Peppi's art club. They are the best part of MY day!

♡ THANK YOU ♡

★ to my husband, **Patrick**, for his unwavering patience and unconditional support during the long months it took to finish this book ♡ (Also, for reminding me to draw Mr. Raccoon 🦝) Thank you for being my rock and my number one fan ♡

★ to my editor, **JuYoun**, for always being there for me through the hard creative periods, the times when I struggled to remember which end of the pen does the writing... Thank you for lighting the way!!

★ to my publisher, **Kurt**, for continuing to take chances on new stories with me and for believing in my work when few people did! THANK YOU ♡

★ to my agent, **Judy**, for always looking out for me and for pushing me in new and exciting directions...

★ to **Melissa and Ru**, two wonderful artists who kindly helped out with colouring the second half of the book ... If it weren't for them, I would have missed my deadline!! FOREVER THANKS ♡

★ to my family and my readers ♡☆♡
I could NOT do what I do without your support. Thank you for reading, thank you for the encouraging words, they make a huge difference in the world of me.''

In gratitude to my dedicated readers I have prepared a small Easter egg hunt for you! If you flip back, you will see Mr. Raccoon 🦝 hiding in some of the chapter panels... Can you find all his cameos?! There are at least 20! ⌣

DESIGN GALLERY

Peppi's character came through in her design almost immediately. I didn't have to agonize over it at all!! She is so fun to draw, especially all her expressions ☺

Peppi (Penelope) Torres

MUNCH MUNCH

pepper

... unlike Jaime, with whose design I reeeally struggled. In the initial sketches his hair was nowhere NEAR the feel I was going for. You know, the kind of hair that won't take crap from anyone, especially a hairbrush. And his character ended up pretty different from what I initially imagined... But that's just how writing goes, sometimes!

Jaime Thompson

I used to sit like that... I never realized how weird it looked, because I was so comfortable

it hurts my legs just to look at you

Jaime Thompson
(science)

Penelope Torres
(art)

Tessa Winston
(art)

Nina Badyal
(art)

Designing all the different characters for this book was the
absolute best part!! They all have little backstories and quirks
and dreams... When I was 11 I really wanted to fly in a spaceship
and visit faraway planets. (Failing that, I wanted to be an animator...)

Maribella Samson
(art)

Jensen Graham
(art)

Felicity Teale
(art)

Nathaniel Tucker
(art

Jenny Yao
(newspaper)

Akilah Salib
(newspaper)

Tyrone Little
(art)

The art and the science club got most of the spotlight in the book, but I really like the newspaper crew characters, and wish I could've shown the adventures that Jenny and Akilah have with THEIR club deadlines...

Derek Lee
(science)

Jack Nielsen
(science)

Leticia Teale
(science)

Sam O'Reilly
(science)
art!

Mr. Ramirez (Mr. R) — art teacher

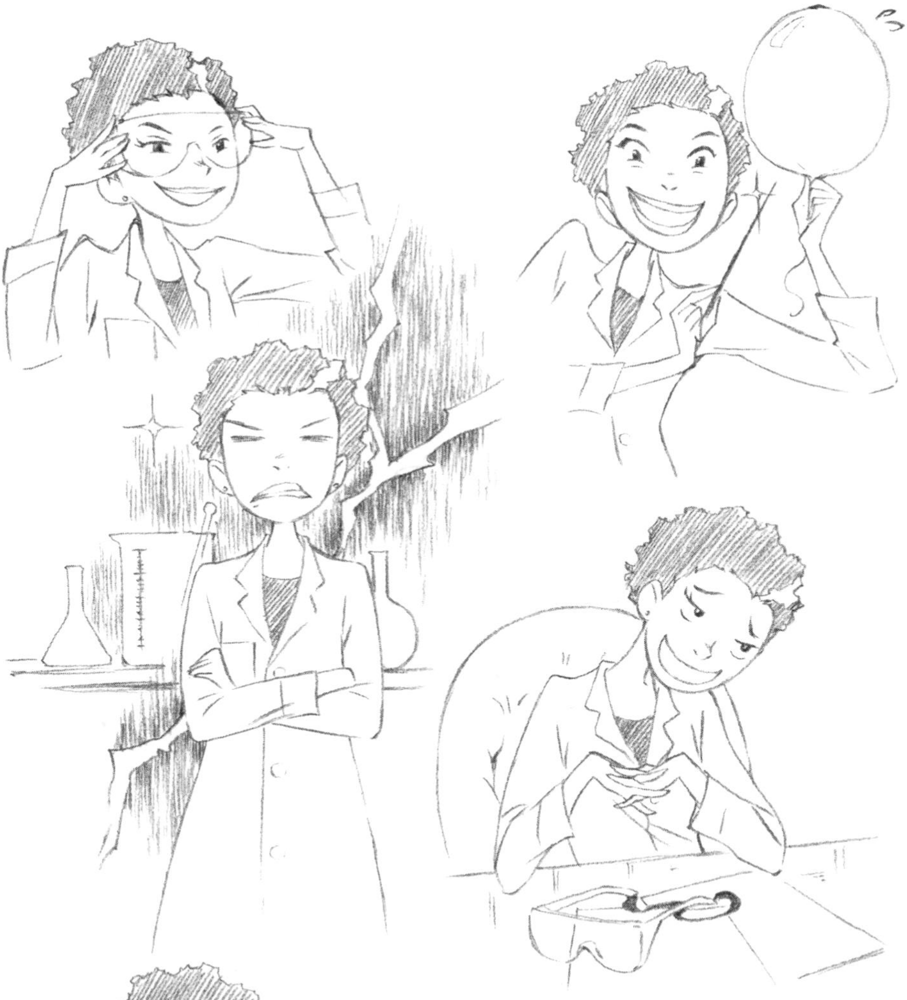

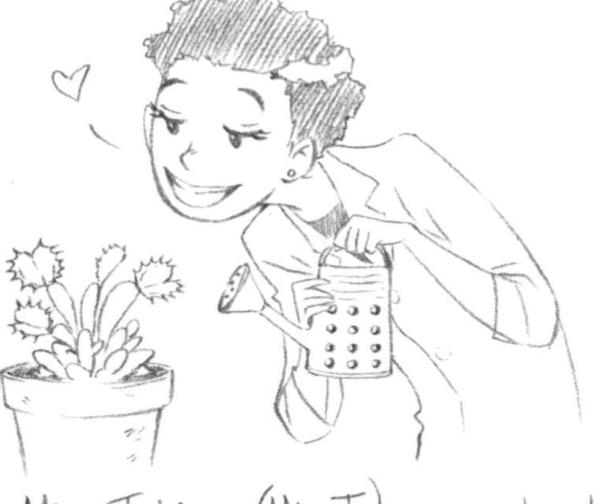

If you asked me to choose between Mr. R and Miss Tobins to pick a favorite, I would cry and ask you why you hate me so much. I love them both!!! They are loosely based on a couple of teachers I had in school (but only very loosely, because I don't want to get sued >_<)

Miss Tobins (Miss T) - science teacher

ART
ROOM!

when designing the club
spaces I tried to imbue them
with the teachers' personalities:

Mr. R is a messy, flighty, creative
soul who still doesn't know how
to check his e-mail (note the cobwebs on
the computers)...

SCIENCE
ROOM:

... while Miss T is the most
logical, ordered person you
would meet. Her classroom is
surgical-table-sparkly CLEAN

DRAWING PROCESS

Like the art club from this book will readily tell you, comics are haaaard... They are a lot of work and take a long time!! Each page in this book took me 6-7 hours to complete. Every creator has their own process, but here is mine:

STEP 1: THE SCRIPT. (Basically a description of action, visual notes and dialogue.)

Page 6

Comically dramatic close-up of Peppi, distraught, draped over her desk: I can't do0o0 it... He probably hates meeee.... I can't face thaaaat...

 Mister Ramirez *tapping on his desk impatiently*: Miss Torres, I did not call this emergency art club meeting to discuss your moral dilemmas!

Mister Ramirez *comically distraught and dramatic*: I have MOST DISTRESSING NEWS.

Jensen *freaked out*: IS IT THE SUNSPOTS, ARE THEY FINALLY—
Mr. R *irritably*: It's NOT the sunspots, Jensen, sit back down!

Mr. R *comically grave*: It's worse. Jensen, in background, comically: w-worse than sunspots...?!

Mr. R: As well you know, each spring this school holds the...

STEP 2: THE STORYBOARDS. (Really really rough, sometimes just stick figure sketches of the page. Here I am blocking in the character posing, layout of the panels, speech balloons and action. I usually draw these on 8.5x11 inkjet paper. It's easy to find!)

STEP 3: THE PENCILS! This penciled page I sketched on regular inkjet paper, with a mechanical pencil. I try to not get too fancy with my tools, in case I lose them... Inkjet paper and a pencil are easily found in many places where humans with desk jobs reside ☺

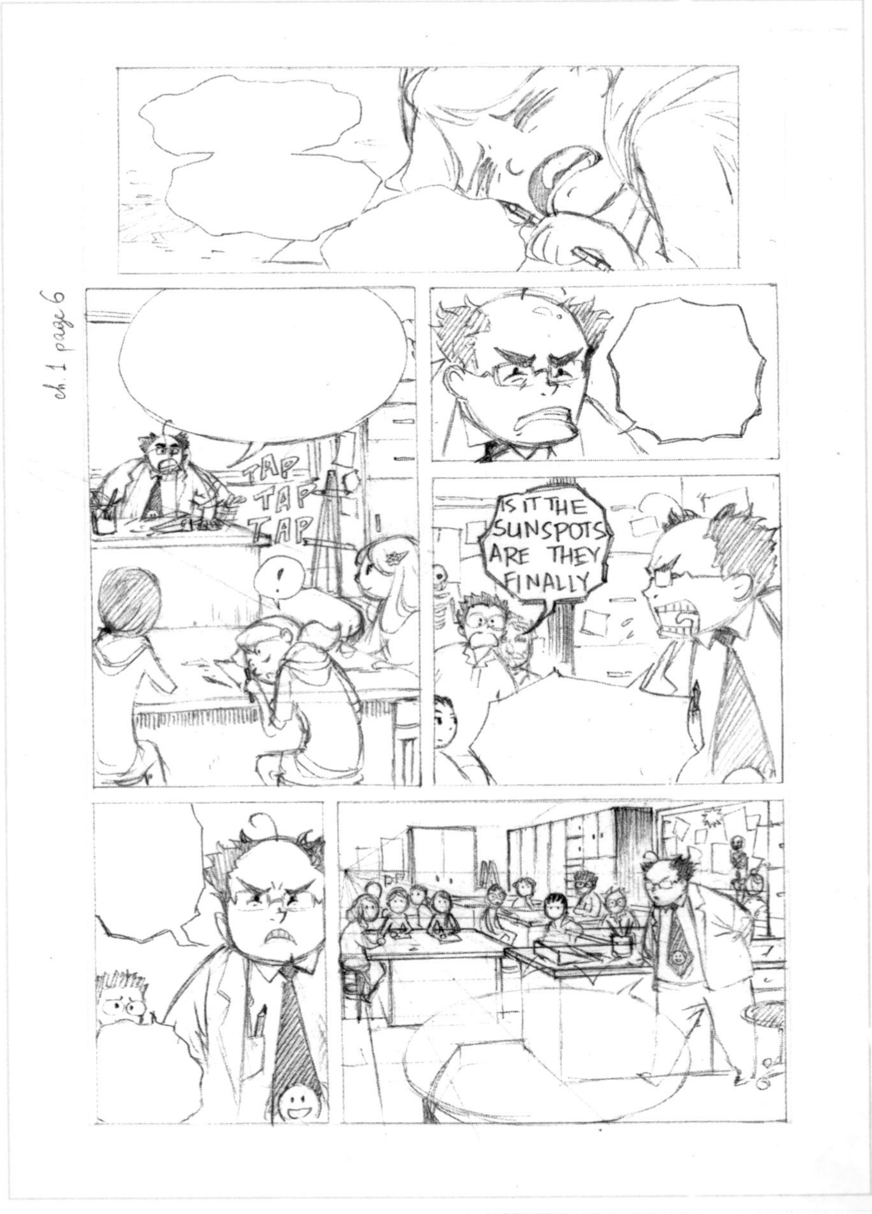
ch. 1 page 6
TAP
TAP
TAP
!
IS IT THE SUNSPOTS ARE THEY FINALLY

STEP 4: INKING!

Many artists will ink right over their sketched pencil lines, but I like to scan my pencils into a graphics program, convert the lines to non-photo blue, then print them out and ink over that (this way I get to keep the penciled pages AND the inked!) The great part about inking over non-photo blue lines, is that when I scan the page in Bitmap/B&W mode, the blue does not show up! So I don't have to do any erasing for the pencil lines!

STEP 5: COLORS!

Once my inked pages are scanned, I use a graphics program to digitally color them! I usually use Photoshop as the graphics software, and a Wacom pen tablet for the drawing input. A long time ago I would use a mouse... But it takes a much longer time and gives you less creative freedom. If you asked me to use it, I would again ask you why you hate me!! ☺

... And there you have it, the magic process that went into the making of this book! ☺
Thank you for reading, and see you aroooound....

Svetlana Chmakova
Apr. 23, 2015

Read more from the halls of Berrybrook Middle School in Svetlana's new books

brave and **crush**!